TREASURE

SEED SAVERS 1

Praise for
TREASURE

"Fast moving and interesting ..."- Willamette Woman Magazine

"I haven't been this in love with a young adult book since Lois Lowry's *The Giver*."- Anakalian Whims Book Blog

"I recommend this book to kids 9+"- Erik, This Kid Reviews Books

"...good for one and all."- Insatiable Readers Blogspot

"brilliant" - Mother Daughter Book Reviews

"With all of the dystopians out these days, it's hard to come across one that is different ..."- Listful Booking

"Engaging and gripping ... I finished it in one sitting." - Jemima Pett, Author of *The Princelings of the East* series

"... an intriguing and frighteningly possible view of a future where seeds ... are no longer legal..."- Caravan Girl

TREASURE

SEED SAVERS 1

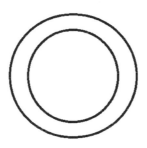

S. Smith

TREASURE
SEED SAVERS 1

Second Edition, 2015
Copyright © 2012 S. Smith
All rights reserved.
ISBN-978-1-943345-03-8

Published by Sandra L. Smith
Cover design and image by Aileen Smith

SUMMARY: In a future where gardening is illegal and Big Brother is always watching, two children set off on a journey to find a place where real food still exists.

1. Juvenile Fiction / Dystopian. 2. Juvenile Fiction / Action & Adventure / Survival Stories. 3. Juvenile Fiction / Nature & the Natural World / Environment.

http://seedsaversseries.com

For all the people who plant seeds every spring.

Other books by S. Smith

Lily (Seed Savers 2)

Heirloom (Seed Savers 3)

28 Days: A Smoky Mountain Christmas (a Seed Savers short story)

The Lunchroom (short stories and poems for the Seed Savers series)

Coming in November 2015:

Keeper (Seed Savers 4)

.

CONTENTS

PART ONE: THE LEARNING

PART TWO: THE GARDEN STATE

PART THREE: JOURNEY TO EDEN

God said,
*"I give you every seed-bearing plant
on the face of the whole earth
and every tree that has fruit with seed in it.
They will be yours for food."*

Genesis 1:29

Part One
THE LEARNING

1

ESCAPE DOWN AN ALLEY

Clare walked faster, clutching the tiny packet to her chest. The sound of the footsteps behind kept pace. She darted down an alley she knew well—turning right, then left, then right again. Standing still, her back against the wall, she listened. The footsteps had not followed her; she had lost them.

Twenty minutes later and safe in the apartment, she met with her co-conspirators: Dante, her seven-year-old brother, and Lily, her best friend.

"I have something to show you, but you have to promise not to tell."

"We promise."

Holding out her closed fist, she whispered, "What I have here will change the world."

Dante's eyes widened. "It's so small."

"It may be small now," she told him, "but what I have in my hand will get bigger. It will grow and

5

make more."

"What is it?" Lily asked.

"Is it magic?" asked Dante.

She opened her hand. In it was a little brown envelope.

Clare tapped the packet lightly, the open end down. Two tiny specks, flat, and tear-shaped, fell into her other hand. They were not much bigger than the head of a pin.

"What is it?" Dante asked.

"Seeds."

"What's 'seeds'?"

"Seeds make food."

Dante's eyes grew round and wide, as did Lily's.

"Get out of here!" Lily cried. "You can't make food. Everyone knows that food comes from Stores and from Delivery Trucks if you have government ration tickets—but people can't *make* food."

Dante laughed. "But wouldn't it be great if people could make food?" he said, grinning widely. "Hey, Lily, it would be like making money. What if we could make as much money as we wanted?"

Lily started to laugh. "Yeah, I could make a million bucks and buy a truckload of Sweeties."

"We wouldn't even need money if we *could* make food," Dante pointed out, doubling over with laughter.

BAM! Clare slammed her fist down on the table, leaving her thumb sticking up. The laughter stopped instantly. Lily and Dante immediately stacked their fists on top of Clare's. The meeting had come back to order.

"People *can* make their own food," Clare said. She picked up the white specks. "These are seeds," she repeated. "They turn into food. These two seeds can make more food than you could eat in a whole day."

Her brother and her friend stared disbelievingly at the specks—the *seeds*.

"How?" they asked.

"I'm not sure," Clare admitted. "I don't know yet. But I'll learn; I'll learn soon. In the meantime, we need to keep the seeds safe."

Dante nodded his head slowly up and down.

"What do you mean?" Lily asked.

"Well," Clare began, her voice lowering, "I don't think regular people are supposed to have seeds. It might not even be legal."

Dante and Lily gasped.

Clare held up her hands. "But even if it is illegal," she said, talking faster now, "it's a dumb law. It's wrong! Everyone should have the right to produce their own food if it's possible. Don't you think so? I mean, why shouldn't we?"

Lily started to say something, but stopped.

"What?" pressed Clare. "Don't you think so?"

"I don't know. I guess I don't get it. If Stores have all the food we need, and if poor people get ration cards for Delivery Trucks, why would anyone need or want to make their own food?"

Clare let out an exasperated sigh. "Lily, I'm still learning. But here's what I know so far. Have you noticed how the people who live mostly on food from ration tickets are more unhealthy than other people?"

"Yeah, sort of. But they're not starving like the ones on the Monitor. In fact, they're kind of fat."

"Exactly. And they often die younger than the people in the big houses and mansions."

"Yeah. But that's the way things are."

"It's the way things are because of food. The food from the Trucks is not the same as the food in Stores. And, Lily, the food from seeds is even better."

2

A VISIT FROM GRIM

hen Clare arrived home from school the next day, her mother was waiting for her at the door.

"Clare, you wanna tell me what's goin' on?"

Clare thought of the seeds safely hidden in her left shoe; she thought about the man who had followed her.

"What, Mama?"

"Some men from GRIM were here to see me today."

"GRIM?"

"The Green Resource Investigation Machine," she said, tossing a business card onto the kitchen table. "They asked if I had a twelve-year-old daughter. I told them I only had a seven-year-old son. Then they showed me a family photo of us together. Right away I looked like a liar. What's going on, Clare?"

"What did you tell them, Mama?"

"What could I tell them? I don't know nothin' 'bout no GRIM. But I didn't like their looks or their attitude. That's why I wasn't cooperative. When they said I had a daughter named Clare who attended St. Vincent Private, and played volleyball for fun, and had a best friend named Lily, I said, 'Why you guys askin' me questions you already know the answers to?'"

Clare flinched.

"Don't you worry, they didn't hurt your mama. They just smiled real insincere like and said that I'd better pay closer attention to where my children are after school. I thanked them for their advice and showed them the door."

Clare sat, silent.

"Well?" her mother asked.

"You really want to know?"

Her mom sighed deeply, that tired-out sigh Clare knew too well. The sigh of a woman who worked two jobs so her children didn't have to eat the food from Trucks and to send them to private parochial school. She turned toward the window, her eyes focused far away.

"No," she answered, almost imperceptibly.

Clare typed GRIM into the search engine.

The Green Resource Investigation Machine was formed thirty-five years ago in an effort to codify and streamline food production in the United States. At the time, most people bought food from larger and larger grocery stores, or "supermarkets" as they were often called.

Originally, food had been grown by individuals and eaten according to the season in which it ripened.

She was having a hard time understanding what she read. How did seasons relate to food? What did "ripen" mean? What did it mean to "grow" food? She continued to read.

Some people grew extra produce to sell and brought their excess "to market." Hence, the later term, "supermarket." The supermarkets gave way to what are currently called "Stores."

The old way of growing, selling, and preserving food was inefficient and cumbersome. It required people to own land and learn all aspects of food production. It wasn't economical, practical, or safe. With the scientific breakthroughs of the late twentieth century, researchers were able to genetically modify seeds, enabling plants to resist disease, insects, and weeds. Techniques were introduced making it possible to grow more food on less land, with less labor, for less cost. Large companies eventually won the right to patent seeds, which had previously been a part of the public domain. The "owners" of the seeds eventually became a part of government policy making.

One of GRIM's main tasks today is to keep track of subversive elements who work against the government's official food policy: anarchists, environmentalists, and seed savers.

Clare gasped. *Seed savers.* Is that what she was now? A seed saver? She had been warned. The old woman who entrusted her with the seeds told her she had to be brave.

She hadn't really believed her. How could she? Who would believe something as tiny as those two seeds could be dangerous?

3

ANA

lare told Lily and Dante about the men from GRIM who had visited their apartment and about being followed in the alley. She shared what she had learned from her limited Monitor search. She said she thought she was being followed whenever she went out.

"Aren't you afraid, Clare?" Lily asked.

"Sort of. But I don't think they'll hurt me. My biggest worry is if they put Mama in jail."

Dante's eyes opened wide.

"I don't see how they can," she added hurriedly. "Mama doesn't know anything. And the seeds are never in the apartment. They couldn't arrest her."

"So," Lily prodded, still curious, "how do the seeds make food? And what kind of food is it?"

"Yeah," Dante asked, licking his lips, "is it Sweeties?"

"I'm not sure," Clare said, furrowing her brow.

"I'm pretty sure it's not Protein. It could be Sweeties. But it sounded more like Vitees. My friend said food is different now than before. She said food used to have a lot of names."

"Like how?" asked Lily.

"Yeah, like how?" repeated Dante.

"Well, like now we have Protein, Sweeties, Vitees, Carbos, and Snacks. They had things called fruit and veg, vegTABLES, and meat, and—oh, I don't remember. It's hard to remember all of the new words. She promised to teach me more and let me write it down. It sounded really interesting. The food in those groups all had individual names, too, and came in different sizes and colors and shapes—"

"—Shapes? What other shapes for food could there be besides square and round?"

"I don't know—I don't really get it. I tried to find out more about it on the Monitor, but that information is blocked."

A secretive look spread across Lily's face. "When will you see her again?" She whispered.

"Soon," Clare whispered back. "I've been dying to, but what with GRIM on my tail, I've been waiting."

Lily and Dante nodded. Dante placed his fist with the thumb up on the table in front of them. The two girls latched on.

On Sunday, Clare and Dante walked seven blocks to St. Vincent Catholic Church. They hurried down a side aisle, stopping four rows from the front. Clare prodded Dante toward the center of the long bench. Several minutes later, an elderly woman made her way into the pew, sliding in next to Clare.

As the congregation sang, the song flowing up around Clare seemed to her a beautiful painting and the individual voices were strokes of color making up the whole. She felt safe and at ease in church.

Dante squirmed through the long service.

"Why do you like church?" he asked as they walked home afterward.

"I like feeling close with God."

"I don't feel close with God in church."

"You will, someday."

"I think it's boring."

Clare glanced around. There was no one close enough to hear. "I first heard about seeds in church."

Dante perked up. "You did?"

"Yes," she answered. "The Bible talks about seeds. Father preached a sermon one day about a man sowing seeds. I didn't understand it, but I noticed the old people were nodding their heads. There eyes were kind of watery like they were about to cry." She turned and looked at Dante. "Did you see the woman who came in after us?"

"Yeah. She always sits there."

"Yes. She does. Her name is Ana."

"You know her name?"

"Be quiet, I'm trying to tell you something. After

the seed sermon, I asked the woman—Ana—about it. She smiled and explained a little about seeds. She asked if I wanted to meet later and learn more. We've met a couple of times since then, in different places."

Clare grabbed his arm and stopped walking. She looked him full in the face. "Dante, she is my friend. Do you understand?"

His eyes showed confusion, but then the light of understanding flashed on. He nodded.

"You can't tell anybody, not even Mama, and especially not strangers. Now keep walking. Someone might be watching."

Once home, Clare took Dante into her room. "Let me show you something." She opened her prayer book and there, among the thin pages, was another small packet. A high-pitched squeak slipped out of Dante's mouth, like air out of a balloon.

"How? When?"

"In church," she said, "during greetings, right into my hand."

He smiled broadly. "You are so smart."

"And," his sister added, "I slipped a letter into Ana's Bible. I requested a meeting so I could ask more questions."

"Can I come?"

"Of course. You, me, and Lily are now signed up for after-school tutoring at St. Vincent's."

4

✳

LESSON AT ST· VINCENT'S

t surprised Clare that GRIM still followed her around. They had nothing on her. She wasn't even sure why they had tailed her in the first place. How could they have known about the seeds? She expected they would soon close their case, and the shadows would disappear.

Until then, she, Lily, and Dante were making a game out of it. They spent many afternoons leading the man—whose veiled attempts to blend in failed miserably—on wild goose chases. It was particularly fun if he was on a bike. They'd pedal fast and go places meant only for children, ending with the GRIM agent panting for breath or covered in mud and swearing.

Most of the time, though, the kids carried on as usual: staying over at each others' homes, riding around on their bikes, and watching the Monitor.

They attended school, church, and after-school tutoring. But Clare didn't let her guard down. There was no way she was going to get anybody in trouble.

On Tuesday afternoon, the children rode their bikes to the church. It had taken a lot of convincing Mama to let Dante ride that distance, but Clare's insistence and promises to keep him close won her over. Mama was pleased with the kids' eagerness to attend free tutoring.

Once inside, Clare spotted Ana right away. She hurried to a table near the back of the large room. Lily and Dante followed.

"Hi, Ana," Clare called.

"Well, hello, dear," the woman answered. "This must be Lily and Dante," she said, smiling at the children.

Clare made introductions and they sat down at the round table. She wasn't sure what to expect. She had told the others that Ana would explain how seeds became food. What she had read on the Monitor had increased her curiosity more than ever, but additional searches had yielded little. She was hoping today would be the day all her questions were answered.

In her fantasy, they would arrive to find a table stacked high with old and dusty books: Books with pictures and stories that would solve the mystery to which she'd been given only crumbs like the pigeons in the courtyard outside.

One lonely book sat atop the table. Clare's heart

sank.

"So," Clare said slowly, "what will we be learning today?"

Ana smiled. "Today, you'll learn about plants."

"Plants!" Dante cried. "I already know about plants."

"Oh, do you, Mr. Dante? Tell me what you know about plants."

"Well," he said, hesitantly, thinking. "Plants are green, and ... they usually grow outside, but Mama used to have an inside plant. It died."

"Very good. Can you name the parts of a plant?"

The two girls sat quietly, their faces betraying their eagerness to answer should Dante fail.

"Um. Leaves?"

"Yes."

"And—roots?"

Ana clapped her hands. "Very good, Dante."

Lily raised her hand.

"Yes, Lily?"

"Isn't that one part called the stem?"

"It sure is," Ana said.

"Um," Clare interrupted, "why are we talking about plants? I know this is after-school tutoring, but I thought ... " she stopped talking.

"Yes?"

She lowered her voice to a whisper. "I thought you were going to teach us about the seeds?"

Ana smiled. "Yes," she said. "I surely am."

Clare was confused. Not only had the discussion so far been about plants, but she had noticed that the book on the table was a Bible.

Ana reached out and picked up the Bible. She opened it to the very beginning. "Gather close, children." The children scooted in.

"Clare," she said in a strong teacher voice. "Please read for us Genesis, chapter one, verses eleven and twelve."

The children looked at each other, perplexed. Lily pushed the plain black book closer to Clare.

Clare cleared her throat and read, "Then God said, 'Let the land produce vegetation: seed-bearing plants and trees on the land that bear fruit with seed in it, according to their various kinds.' And it was so. The land produced vegetation: plants bearing seed according to their kinds and trees bearing fruits with the seed in it according to their kinds. And God saw it was good." She stopped reading and looked up.

"Well," said Ana, looking from face to face. "I think there might be some words in this passage that you don't know—yes?"

Dante looked eagerly at the older girls. They were nodding their heads. He joined in.

"Veg—e—ta—tion?" Clare asked. "It sounds sort of like the 'vegeTABLE' word you told me about that time."

"Yes," replied Ana, "very good—*vegetable*," she pronounced correctly, "and *vegetation* are word relatives. In this case vegetation means all kinds of plants and trees. What else?"

"Fruit?" Lily offered. She was thinking of the discussion she'd had some days before with Clare. This was one of the words that had come up.

"Ah, yes, fruit," Ana said. "Well?" She looked at them sternly. "Take out a piece of paper!"

They snapped to it and bustled into their bags for paper and pencils.

"You may draw pictures," she said to Dante. "Fruit is another part of the plant." She paused while the girls scribbled down what she'd said. "Let's all draw a picture."

Ana drew a plant, labeling the parts. It was something the older girls had done in school. "Fruit," Ana explained, as she added a large blob to her drawing, "is a part of the plant people nowadays have forgotten about."

Lily's forehead wrinkled. "No one ever mentioned that before," she said.

"I've never seen a fruit on a plant," Dante added.

After the children added fruit to their plant pictures, Ana asked Lily to read the Bible verses Clare had read earlier. Afterward she asked them what was inside of the fruit.

"Seeds," Dante hollered so loud the three females shushed him at once.

The children felt as if they'd discovered something significant: seeds came from fruit, which came from plants. Even though they couldn't remember having seen anything like a fruit, they all knew about plants. Plenty of bushes and trees grew in the city—or at least on the outer edges of the city. But they still were not sure what any of this had to do with food.

Clare was finally brave enough to pose the question.

"So what's this got to do with food?"

Ana looked at her blankly.

Clare tried again. Maybe the old woman hadn't heard her. "What does seeds coming from fruit and plants have to do with food?"

Ana faltered. "What do plants have to do with food?" she repeated.

"Yeah," the three children said, nodding.

"Oh dear," Ana said, speaking only to herself. "It's worse than I thought."

5

DANTE DISCOVERS FRUIT

na was about to explain what apparently the children lacked in basic botanic knowledge when they realized the room had emptied.

"Oh," she said. "It looks like our time is up. We'll have to pick up the question next time. In the meantime, do try to study your new words. I know it's not much, but it's a start. I'll see you in a couple days."

When the kids arrived back at Clare and Dante's place, they headed straight for Clare's room. Though small, the apartment had three tiny bedrooms. Actually, Dante's room wasn't a room at all. Mama had found office cubicle partitions at a local thrift store and walled off a part of the living room for Dante. Since Clare was almost a teenager, Mama didn't think it was appropriate for the two children to continue sharing a room. All three of them had decorated the dividers with butcher paper and drawings of dinosaurs; Dante was proud to "move in." Clare loved the new-found space in her room formerly occupied by Dante's small bed. Someday soon she hoped to get a desk or bean bag chair. For now, she delighted in the fact that she had a space in the world to call her own.

The children took out their drawings, flung themselves across Clare's bed, and contemplated what they'd heard from Ana that day.

"Have you ever seen a plant with a fruit on it?" Lily asked Clare.

"No, and we never learned it in school, either."

"I have," said Dante.

"You have??" the two girls exclaimed. "But you're only in second grade."

"No, I mean, I've seen a fruit."

"You have??" they said again.

"I didn't think I had, but after a while I remembered something." He jumped off the bed and darted out of the room. He returned carrying a box of Juice.

"See?" he said. "In this picture. There are trees. And see these little colored things? I think that's supposed to be fruit."

The girls took the box from him and squinted their eyes, looking closer.

"I think he's right," Lily said. "There are definitely some colored circles here. They don't look like leaves."

"Hmm," said Clare, looking up. "I guess I never noticed that before. D'ya think?"

Dante smiled, pleased with his discovery. "I found fruit," he sang. "I found fruit."

"Still," his sister said, "it's only a picture; it's not real."

Her skepticism wasn't enough to dampen Dante's mood.

"I still want to know how seeds make food," Clare said. She tried working it out. "Okay, we know that seeds are found in fruit, and seeds make food, but how do seeds make food, and where is this fruit that holds all these seeds? And why is it against the law to have seeds? That must be why we never see plants with fruit, because the seeds would be everywhere. Arrghh," she screamed. "My head is going to explode!"

"Oh no," Lily shouted, "her head is going to explode! Quick, Dante, let's soften the explosion with pillows!"

Dante and Lily piled pillows onto the struggling Clare until they all exhausted themselves with laughter.

6

ANA'S REFLECTION

ow long had it been, Ana thought to herself, since real food had appeared on store shelves? She counted the years and thought of the children. It had easily been gone for the entirety of their short lives.

And the backyard gardens had disappeared even sooner—especially in cities. Why, urban gardens had been an oddity even when she was a child. It didn't take much reflection to understand how the children had no concept of food originating from plants. The only function of plants they knew was purely ornamental; the only concept of food was something chopped, pressed, cut, and wrapped tightly in plastic, and neatly packed in square boxes. Food so unlike the original source that it bore no resemblance to a plant and held little of the original nutritional value.

Of course, the current food was supposedly pumped full of vitamins and nutrients, but was it the same? And what else was it pumped full of to give it the shelf life needed to be sold from Stores?

Ana shook her head, thinking about the way things were now, compared to the old days. She wondered if humankind could ever make its way back. The old woman walked slowly to her bedroom. She pulled out the top left drawer of her dresser—the one with the false bottom. She lifted the folded clothing out of the drawer and set it aside. Carefully, she slid the thin wooden board out of its place to reveal the tiny square compartments. Her eyes gazed lovingly at the seeds filling each section. The larger seeds—beans, corn, and peas—occupied the cubicles. The smaller seeds—tomatoes, peppers, lettuce, basil and such—were tucked into the paper envelopes.

Ana wasn't sure how much longer she would be around to secretly grow the herbs and vegetables she raised each year, eating some of the treasured produce, but more importantly, saving the seeds. Besides those she had grown herself, she stored seeds from other Seed Savers who met once a year to exchange seeds—a traveling Noah's Ark of food.

Seed Savers, a secret society whose initial goals were to salvage seeds and skills before they were lost, had hopes of changing the policies and politics governing the nation's food supply. Someday, the people would come to their senses about food, and when that day arrived, there would be pure seeds left with which to begin again.

Ana thought about the children. She knew she was putting them in danger by giving them seeds and teaching them, but what kind of a future was she passing on if she *didn't* share her knowledge and her seeds?

7

"GOOD FOR FOOD"

he children arrived early for their second
tutoring session and immediately spied Ana
sitting at a table reading her Bible. They
rushed over to her.

"Oh, there you are," she said as they yanked the
chairs from the table. She closed the Bible and set it
aside. "How is everyone today?"

After a few minutes of chit chat, she proceeded to
quiz them on the definitions of words such as
"vegetation" and "fruit" and asked for examples.
They easily came up with examples for vegetation,
but were still stumped by fruit.

"We've never seen a plant with fruit. We looked,
but there wasn't anything like this on any of the trees
and plants around our apartment building," Clare
said, pointing toward her sketch of the fruited plant
she'd made at their last session.

"Oh," Lily said, "remember what Dante found?"

29

Ana looked at the children, her eyebrows raised in question.

"Well," Clare hesitated, "I'm not sure that was real."

"Yeah," cried Dante, "tell her, tell her: I found a picture of fruit—on the Juice box!"

Clare smiled apologetically at Ana. "On the Juice box, there was this picture of trees and on the trees were these colored circles ... Dante thought it looked like fruit."

Ana nodded, her eyes glistening. "Yes," she said, "Dante is right. Those are fruit."

"Yes!" Dante shouted.

"So," Clare ventured, "last time you were about to explain the connection between plants and food."

Ana smiled, nodding. "Oh yes," she answered. "A very important point, to be sure." She picked up the Bible and handed it to Lily. "Your turn, dear. Genesis 1: 29, please."

Lily opened the floppy book. Clare helped her locate the verse.

"Then God said, 'I give you every seed-bearing plant on the face of the whole earth and every tree that has fruit with seed in it. They will be yours for food.'"

A moment of silence followed the reading.

"I don't get it," Clare finally said. "What is ours for food? The seeds?"

"Can you read it again, please, Lily?" Ana

instructed.

Lily read again, "Then God said, 'I give you every seed-bearing plant on the face of the whole earth and every tree that has fruit with seed in it. They will be yours for food.'" Lily paused, "It sounds like you can eat the plants and the fruits from the trees."

"Bingo!" Ana said.

Dante laughed. "People can't eat plants."

"How can you eat a plant?" asked Lily.

"Aren't they poisonous?" said Clare.

"Maybe we should read a little more. Lily, pass the Bible to Clare. Clare, Genesis 2:8."

"Now the Lord God had planted a garden in the east, in Eden; and there he put the man he had formed. And the Lord God made all kinds of trees grow out of the ground—trees that were pleasing to the eye and good for food—"

"That's good," Ana said. "Stop there."

"Wow," said Dante, "if the trees are good for food, the fruit must be okay to eat."

"Okay, okay," Clare said, "but that doesn't say the *plants* are good for food."

"Dear, the plants are good for food—but it's not the way you're thinking—just wait, I'll teach you."

Lily had taken the Bible back and was quietly rereading the last verse.

"Anything the matter, Lily?" Ana asked.

The girl looked up. "It says here that the Lord God planted a *garden*? It sounds like my last name."

"Oh yeah, I noticed that, too," said Clare. "And I've seen that word on the Monitor."

Dante was barely listening now. On the paper in front of him he had drawn tree after tree, each bearing round fruits of various colors. In the sky was a big face.

Ana gazed at Lily. "Lily Gardener, what a marvelous name. 'Lily'—a most beautiful and fragrant flower. And 'Gardener'—one who tends, or takes care of a garden. A garden," she said, "is a place where plants and trees are planted and cared for. It can be a flower garden or a vegetable garden. A place of beauty and rest, or a simple plot for food-bearing plants. A garden is *intentional*," she said with finality.

"Is it sort of like a park or a botanical reserve?" asked Clare.

"Yes. The botanical reserves are what we have left. I'm not sure when the word 'garden' fell out of favor. I think it was around the time seed saving was outlawed. It was better for the corporations, agri-business, those who wanted society to forget the concept of growing food by and for oneself. They took away our means to do it, made laws forbidding it, and changed the language to erase our memory of it."

The children were silent. Then the girls began scribbling furiously in their notebooks, writing down everything Ana had told them.

Dante simply began adding letters across the sky of his picture. G-A-R-D-E-N right between the tops of the fruit trees and God's face.

8

BURIED TREASURE

fter the girls wrote down an explanation of "garden" and that plants were food, they begged Ana to tell them more about what it meant to grow a food plant.

"I've been thinking about this," Ana answered. "It's hard to know where to start."

"Start at the beginning!" Dante said.

"Or perhaps the ending, and work back," Ana teased.

"No, please, the beginning," Lily begged.

"Very well, then." Ana reached for the Bible.

The children sighed. Clare couldn't help it. Though she'd been raised to show respect for adults and went to church most every Sunday, she was baffled as to why the only book Ana brought was a Bible.

"Ana, I think reading about plants in the Bible is great." Clare hesitated. "But we were kind of hoping you had some old books." She lowered her voice, "books about plants and fruits and seeds. Books with big pictures."

Dante nodded eagerly.

"Well now," Ana said, letting go of the Bible. "Sounds to me like you need to hear some of the ending after all."

The kids scrunched up their faces.

Ana's voice was low. "There certainly were such books—are still. But they aren't easy to find. The large food lobby, with the government's backing, has taken them out of circulation. If I had these books, do you think it would be wise for me to tote them all over here and show them to you? Not only could I lose the books and be charged large fines, if GRIM found out I was teaching agriculture to children, I could be imprisoned."

The children's eyes grew wide.

"If, on the other hand, a little old lady like me carries a Bible in and out of church, nobody is suspicious." She turned to Clare. "Does that answer your question?"

"Yes," she said. "I'm sorry, Ana. I'm just so curious to find out more. Ever since you started bringing me the seeds and hinting about making food, I've wanted to know everything."

"Is fruit as pretty as on the juice box?" Dante asked.

Ana smiled, her face erupting in wrinkles. "In

fact, Dante, it's even better."

"Wow."

Ana sighed. "Well, if you must know everything all at once, I suppose it wouldn't hurt to tell you quickly, and we can do the actual studying and note-taking later. We haven't much time left today. Remind me what you already know."

The children took turns spewing out bits of knowledge, but like an incomplete jigsaw puzzle, many pieces were missing. What they knew was this: Seeds could turn into food. Seeds came from fruit, and fruit came from plants (though they had never actually seen fruit on a plant). Plants could somehow be eaten (though they had never eaten a plant, nor had they ever known anyone who had eaten a plant). Food came from Stores or Trucks, was usually square or round, came in a few colors, and followed the basic groups of Proteins, Carbos, Vitees, Sweeties, and Snacks.

"And so you want to know how those seeds I gave you turn into a Sweetie, or a Protein, or a Vitee?"

"Yes!"

"Ana," Dante said, "I think I know. I saw it on a cartoon once. You put the seed in a dish and add water. Pop!" he said, his hands expanding.

The girls looked hopefully at Ana.

"Good guess," she said. "But it's not quite that easy. In fact, it's rather hard work. But not unenjoyable. Many people loved growing their own

36

food. And, mmm, that food, *real* food, tastes *so* good. People nowadays are so used to this other kind of *stuff* ... I'm not sure they would even appreciate good food. No, no," it was as if she were arguing with herself, "of course they would. Especially the fresh herbs. Oh, and the fruit: apples, oranges, pineapples, peaches, plums. Oh Dante," she held his hands. "If you could pick fruit ripened on the tree, not those silly kind the supermarkets used to sell, and bite into it—something really sweet and juicy— maybe a really juicy apple, a big crunch and then juice running down your chin. Or a peach," she was nearly ranting now, "a fresh, ripe, yellow peach. Oh what I wouldn't give for a peach." Her voice trailed off.

"What's a peach?" Dante asked.

"A peach is like eating sunshine. The flesh is a bright, deep yellow, or soft pink—smooth, and velvety. It's a Sweetie and Juice and summer all at once. It's heaven."

"Wow," the small boy said reverently. "I hope those seeds Clare has make peaches."

"I'm afraid not," Ana said. "A lot of fruit comes from trees, and trees would be hard to hide. Berries— melons, possibly—but most fruit we will have to dream about for the future. Anyway, where was I?"

"You were telling us that turning a seed into food was hard work, but that some people liked the work," Clare said.

"And that the food you make from seeds tastes better than the food we have now," Lily added.

"Oh, yes, precisely, that's where I got carried away." She raised her white eyebrows and smiled.

Ana reached down and pulled something from the pocket of her sweater. She rested her closed fist on the table and opened it slowly like a flower opening its petals to the sunshine. Three small capsules were inside. They were hard and white, with little black eyes.

"What is it?" Dante asked. "Fruit?"

"Seeds!" Ana said.

Stunned cries came from the children.

"But they don't look like the other seeds you gave me," Clare said.

"That's true. I've only brought you small seeds, ones that were easy to pass. These are bean seeds," she said, placing one in each child's hand. "They're one of my favorites to watch grow. Now listen while I explain the process. We're almost out of time." The children listened, holding the precious seeds tightly.

"To grow food, you bury the seed in soil. The seed needs water to begin growing, to sprout; germination it's called. After a certain amount of time, if the soil is warm enough and the seed stays moist, a plant will grow from within the seed, pushing up through the soil."

She paused, checking the children's faces for comprehension. "Each seed contains within it a complete plant and everything the plant needs to grow."

Dante broke the silence that followed. "So it's all there in the seed? The whole plant is just waiting inside the seed? It's like a treasure that you need to bury instead of one that you dig up?"

"So it is, Dante, so it is."

"Then what?" Lily prodded, trying to get to the bottom of things.

"Well, the plant grows bigger and bigger if it continues to have light and water. Some plants produce a fruit containing seeds. Other plants will just make more seed. And so it goes. You already know the other parts of the plant. People ate various plants, and different parts of each plant. Sometimes the preferred part is the leaves, sometimes it's the root, or stem—"

"—Eww—"

"Other times it's the fruit, or even the seed."

"People eat the seeds?"

"Look at your bean seeds—beans are very popular food in many parts of the world—and used to be here."

"But they're so small," said Lily.

"And hard," added Dante.

Ana laughed. "You make them soft," she explained. "And you eat a whole pile of them," she said, looking at Lily.

"Oh."

She sensed their hesitation.

"So that's it?" Clare said. "You bury the seeds in soil and they grow into plants, and you eat the plants? How long does it take?"

"It takes time." She could tell Clare was disappointed. But what could she expect? These children were used to instant food, instant information, ready-made everything. Still, she knew the desire was there. Be patient, she told herself. Bring them along carefully. Children are our only hope.

9

❦

CARROTS ARE ROOTS!

On their next visit, the children brought their math textbooks. Ana had suggested it would look more natural to have school books scattered about the table.

They were excited. Today she had promised to teach more about vegetables. They had really enjoyed hearing about the juicy, sweet, good-as-summer fruit Ana had described. But she explained that eventually they would be growing food and saving seeds, and since most fruits grew on sizable bushes or trees, it was better to focus on vegetables and herbs. They had added the new words and definitions before leaving on their last visit. Now they were ready to learn.

As usual, they started with reading from the Bible. They read from 2 Samuel 17, about how the people were hungry in the desert and the kind of food they brought along. Among the foods mentioned were beans, the very seed Ana had shown them last time. Then they read about vegetables called cucumbers and onions. Ana explained about each of these plants, how they grew, and which parts were eaten. The children took notes and sketched from Ana's examples. They still had a hard time fathoming how you'd ever eat a root. It was bad enough to consider a leaf or a stem, but a root?

"Clare," she said, "you do still have the first packet of seeds I gave you?"

"Yes, of course."

"And the second?"

The girl nodded her head.

"Did you look inside the packets?"

"Yes."

"Were the seeds the same?"

"No. The seeds in the second packet were even smaller than the first."

"Those are for a vegetable called carrot. Carrots are the root of the plant."

The children didn't know what to say, so said nothing.

Ana borrowed two of Dante's crayons and began drawing a picture. She drew a long, orange triangle with a branching, green top. "Carrot," she said.

"Where is the root?" Lily asked.

"This orange part is the root!" Ana exclaimed. She pulled a brown crayon from the box and drew a line between the green and orange parts of the carrot.

"Here, the ground is here." She tapped her crayon on the brown line. "At the right time, you pull the carrot out of the ground. You eat this part—the root."

"Do you cook it?" Lily asked.

Ana moved her head slightly from side to side. "It can be eaten cooked or raw," she said, "either way."

"Wow," said Dante. "Just like that, out of the ground? No Store, no microwave? No sauce?"

"Oh, like all food, you can do a lot with it to increase its flavor, but yes, you can eat a carrot just plain, right out of the ground."

"Sooo," Clare surmised. "We are going to be growing carrots?"

Ana smiled and nodded.

"Cool," said Dante.

Each child scrawled the word "carrot" in their notebooks along with their own labeled sketches, being careful to color it just right.

"Ana," Clare asked, before going home, "when will we plant the seeds?"

"Soon, dear one. Soon."

10

A GRIM HISTORY

Ana knew the time was coming when she must move beyond the pleasant task of teaching, and clearly tell the children the risks involved. She felt certain they would want to continue, but it was important they fully understand the path ahead. After that, she would provide detailed instructions on seed sowing, tending, and harvesting. Eventually, she'd set them up with other Seed Savers and bequeath all of her seeds to their care. At times, she worried they were too young.

There was so much to do.

The old woman took her calendar off the wall. Very soon it would be time to plant the first seeds. Maybe they need only plant a few this year. Yes, of course; they should proceed cautiously. One could never be too careful.

It had been years since Ana was cited for home gardening. Thankfully, neither her seeds nor her books had been found, but all the herbs and vegetables were confiscated or ripped from the ground. She had claimed she thought the cilantro, turnips, and chard sprouting throughout her small yard were inedible weeds that had gained a foothold in her landscaping. Indeed, they looked the part.

Up until the raid, Ana had grown illegal plants for years without a problem. Since then, she'd been more careful. She grew most plants indoors now, and sometimes scattered a few seeds in empty lots around town, collecting the seeds later in the season. She wanted to keep as many fresh seeds as possible. It was all part of being a Seed Saver.

And now she was doing the last thing Seed Savers did: teaching someone younger to carry it forward until the dawn of a new day, a day when the old ways of gardening were no longer unlawful. She sighed deeply, thinking of the task in front of her, and of the looming shadow on the land: GRIM.

Although it was GRIM now—an actual arm of the government—it had started earlier with private corporations: BENAR, Nipungyo, Qubceq. Some pointed to the Supreme Court ruling of 1980 okaying the patenting of living organisms as the beginning of the end.

A prediction was made around the turn of the century that if Nipungyo had its way, no farmer in the country, perhaps even the world, would ever own a seed again. It was a prediction that had since gained federal authorization in several nations, and it applied to everyone, not just farmers. All sanctioned seeds in America were genetically enhanced and patented. Owning, purchasing, and planting of all seeds was controlled by the government. The average person knew nothing about growing his or her own food.

Ana shook her head. The average person wouldn't recognize food beyond Vitees, Sweeties, Carbos, Proteins, and Snacks.

She thought back to how it all began. The loss of freedom in gardening and farming was gradual, and started—or so it appeared—innocently enough. Scientists created biotec, or genetically modified seeds, to improve crop production: seeds whose plants were resistant to drought, disease, and insect damage; seeds that produced plants with larger fruit and longer shelf life. Chemical companies created seeds whose plants survived their herbicides, making it easier for farmers to produce a clean and weed-free crop.

The innovations seemed to benefit everybody: the farmer, third world countries, consumers. Like vaccinations or pasteurized milk contributing to the good of humanity, biotec plants were heralded as an improved way of food business. One difference, however, was the ownership rights. A few large corporations, and one in particular—Nipungyo—soon had a corner on the market of genetically modified seeds.

A tear rolled down Ana's face as she recalled the way it had played out. The first to go were small farmers who didn't buy into GM seeds; they had no interest in Nipungyo's herbicides or high-priced seeds. They continued to farm as they always had, by saving seeds from each year's crop to plant in the coming year. Gradually, however, neighboring farms switched to Nipungyo's *Bull's Eye* resistant seeds and cross-pollination occurred. Nipungyo sent representatives out to gather and test seeds; some called them the "seed police." Farmers who'd never used the biotec seeds were run out of business because they didn't have the money to defend themselves.

Consumers also lost. They lost the ability to choose the kind of food they would eat. While some were aware that supermarket food came from genetically modified seeds, most were not. Had they known, they might not have cared, lulled as they were into trusting that somebody else was watching out for them.

People forgot the flavor of food so fresh from the earth you could taste the richness or desperation of the soil in which it was grown. Plants that historically offered untold diversity—such as more

than three thousand varieties of potatoes in Peru—
were bred down to what the seller deemed best,
based on the demand from large chain stores and
"fast food" restaurants. The valued traits of the
chosen monoculture had to do with size,
proliferation, ease of shipping, shelf life, and cost,
rather than flavor or nutrition.

Food became a commodity rather than the
nourishment of life.

Ana recalled how the efforts of small grassroots
groups came too late. By then, corporations had
gained a foothold in key government offices. The
food poisoning outbreaks of the 2010s and 2020s put
fresh market growers out of business and handed all
food growing and production over to agribusiness.
Though never proven, many suspected the food
contamination was intentional so that the
government could finally wrest control from the
people.

Within ten years, only authorized producers were
allowed to grow food. GRIM was formed to enforce
and investigate all things related to food production.
The revolving door of the past between Nipungyo
executives and federal government positions was at
last solidified into one single agency.

11

TOMATOES

Again the children brought their math books to St. Vincent's.

Four books lay on the table. The children tried to hide their disappointment when they saw the letters B-I-B-L-E handwritten neatly across each of the handmade book jackets.

Ana's face shone with joy and mischief. "I thought it would be nice if we could all read together."

Dante began turning pages. Large colorful pictures of plants and trees, and things he'd never seen before, lay before him.

"Look!" he shouted. "My Bible has pictures!"

Lily and Clare were paging through their books. "Hey—wait a minute—"

The girls looked up at Ana, whose smile stretched tight the sagging skin around her mouth, and sent out wrinkles from the corners of her eyes like rays of sunshine.

"Never underestimate what you might find inside a plain brown wrapper," she said winking. "It's risky, but if ever you're to see these books, I figured this would be our best chance. Though you must be careful when others come near. Now let's get these math books of yours lying about." She opened the two textbooks nearest her. "You never know what other people might think or do."

The two girls exchanged glances. Ana's tone was serious. Suddenly they were reminded of the man, who on occasion, still followed them. Meeting here, like this, had begun to feel normal, safe, like real after-school lessons. They had almost forgotten their course of study was forbidden. Yes, forbidden fruit, Clare thought, just like in the Bible.

"Clare, Lily, Dante," Ana said. "Today I'm going to tell you about tomatoes." The children opened their notebooks.

"Tomato: t—o—m—a—t—o," Ana spelled. They copied down the word and waited for more.

"Put down your pencils," she instructed. They stared at her in disbelief, clutching their pencils.

"Down," she repeated. "First, I want you just to listen."

They set their pencils down and looked at Ana.

"A tomato is the fruit of the plant, scientifically speaking. It contains the seeds. In terms of the old 'food groups' we'll call it a vegetable. What I mean is

—it's not sweet like a dessert, a Sweetie, such as fruit from a tree."

"Like a peach!" Dante interrupted.

"That's right. But tomatoes do have many wonderful qualities like other fruits. For example, tomatoes can be eaten raw or cooked. They can be made into sauce and juice. They can be canned, frozen, or dried. Tomatoes come in several colors, but mostly bright red. They're usually round and can be small or large. They are rather soft and very juicy. The seeds are easy to save."

The children, with their limited experience, understood only about half of this, but seemed impressed. They hoped Ana would soon let them write it all down.

"Are they difficult to grow?" asked Lily.

"Not really," answered Ana. "Quite easy." She whispered, "And they can be grown indoors. Though they do get rather large. But oh, so much food, from one tiny seed. You see, unlike a carrot seed, a tomato seed produces a plant with many, many fruits on it."

"Oh, I get it," said Clare.

Dante bravely asked, "Do you think we could get one of those seeds?"

"You already have, dear, you already have."

The children were terribly excited to finally discover that the first seeds Clare brought home were tomatoes. And soon they would be growing their own tomato plants. After Ana surprised them with the news, she surprised them even further by showing them pictures of tomatoes in the brown-papered gardening books.

The remainder of class trickled away as the children drank in the books, examining the many illustrations of vegetable plants and fruit trees.

Whoever said a picture is worth a thousand words must have been thinking of them. Their hearts sang as they carried their treasures home.

They could almost taste the tomatoes.

12

PREPARATION

During their third week together, Ana gave the children extensive notes on how to plant and grow the tomato and carrot seeds. Clare and Dante told her they owned a large pot—leftover from the many ill-fated houseplants their mother had unsuccessfully attempted to grow. Ana judged by their gestures that the size would work just fine for a tomato.

They planned to ask their mom to buy potting soil and tell her it was for a science project—not really a lie, depending on how you looked at it. They would do everything in Clare's room, and Mama would soon forget about it—just like she had forgotten about the philodendron. Because the seeds were precious, they'd plant only one. If it didn't come up after a given number of days, they'd plant the second one; otherwise, it would be saved.

The plan for the carrot seeds was even more

exciting. They would plant dozens of the seeds outside in the loose soil recently left behind by a torn-out hedge. They studied photos in the books so they'd recognize the carrots once they emerged.

"Don't worry," Ana told them. "Carrots take a long time to come up. When they finally do, they're little slivers of green. They're slow starters, but worth the wait. Just make sure the ground isn't too hard, and pull the weeds to give them room."

"Are there any questions?" Ana asked as the children finished their notes. Her question was met by contented silence.

"Well, then I suppose you won't mind a little quiz," she said.

"A quiz?!"

Ana chuckled at the children's concern. "All right, maybe not an actual test. How about a quick review?

"Can we use our notes?" Clare asked.

"Hmm … Yes, you may use your notes since you're just beginning … but there may come a time when you need the knowledge tucked deep in here," she said, tapping her head with her finger.

"First question: What will your seed need to grow?"

"I know," said Lily, "water and warmth, and soil, of course."

"Very good. And once it germinates?"

"Light," they all shouted together.

"Yes, good."

She asked about planting and tending. The children answered nearly every question perfectly. At last Ana asked, "Why must you be careful where you keep your tomato plant?"

"Light!" Dante shouted.

"Dante, I mean besides light. Why must you keep it hidden? And why do you need to be careful about constantly checking for the carrots?"

Clare said, "GRIM," and the smiles slid off their faces.

"That's right, children. I know we've spoken of it before, but I have to say it again. You can still change your minds—" the children looked stricken—"you can back out now. Possessing seeds and growing plants is against the law. I think it's a bad law, but you are children and I hate to involve you in something illegal. Lily, Clare, I think you are old enough to understand what you are doing; Dante, you are very young, and I'm sorry we are burdening you with such a heavy obligation—"

"It's okay, Ana," Clare said. "It's my fault that Dante is in it with us. But you have to understand, I couldn't do this without Dante or Lily. We're the Three Musketeers."

Clare put her hand on the table, thumb up. Lily and Dante joined. Ana had seen them do this time and again. This time she added her wrinkled fist to the top.

"It's okay," Clare repeated. "We're ready."

13

"IT'S TIME"

Finally the day came when Ana told them it was time.

"Do you have the pot with soil ready?"

"Oh, yes," cried Dante. "We bought the dirt weeks ago. Mama has already forgotten about it."

"Good," said Ana. "Because it's time. Remember, plant the carrot seeds very carefully. Just sprinkle them over soil that you've scratched out a bit. Throw a little potting soil over them, firm down, and water gently. Make sure no one is watching. The tomato seed also needs tender care. It will grow best if it's warm, so put it some place toasty if you can."

It was hard to keep their attention for the remaining hour. They were restless and giddy; too excited to learn anything new. Ana understood their excitement, and shared in it. She, too, would plant her normal crops. Although she never knew anymore, whether she would be there for the harvest, she always planted—how could she not?

Planting in spring was part of the rhythm of her life.

She hadn't told the children about her cache of saved seeds or that she intended to pass the bulk of the savings on to them. She would stash away this news for next time, like she stashed away the seeds. There would be the days spent waiting for the seeds to germinate, and that would be a good time to break the next bit of exciting news.

Clare, Dante, and Lily could hardly wait to reach the apartment. One lone man still followed them occasionally, but they were unfazed. He couldn't read their minds, after all. And they had already managed to bring a number of gardening books from church to their homes over the past couple of weeks, so they were feeling invincible.

Back at Clare and Dante's place, the children made a beeline to Clare's room and closed the door. Lily opened her notebook and began reading the instructions they had copied from Ana. In the kitchen, Dante found measuring cups and spoons. They would need utensils to get the soil into the abandoned philodendron pot. Eventually, the pot was filled nearly to the top with soil.

"We should have put some paper down," Clare said, shaking her head at the dirt on the carpet.

"Oh, well," said Lily. "Next time we know."

Silence settled around them like snowfall. They knew what came next—placement of the seed into the soil.

"I feel like we should have a ceremony or something," Dante said.

"A blessing," said Clare.

"Too bad we don't have the Bible," Lily said.

Dante furrowed his brow. "I think Mama has a Bible."

"Nuh-uh," said Clare. "She never goes to church."

"No, really. I think she does." He ran out of the room. After a few minutes he returned, a dusty, dilapidated book in his hands.

"See?"

Clare wiped the dust off the soft cover and opened it up. "Holy Bible," she read. She looked up. "I didn't know Mama had a Bible. How did you know?"

"I saw her write in it when Daddy died."

Clare turned a few more pages. There were pages to record births and deaths. There, printed neatly, she read their birth dates. She also saw the name of her father, the record of his birth and death, and the marriage of her parents. It brought back memories of happier—and sadder—times. She slammed the book shut before a tear slipped out of her eyes.

"A blessing?" Lily reminded her.

"Oh, yes," Clare said, collecting herself. "Where is that part about God declaring all of the food in the garden good?"

"It was right at the beginning: Genesis." She took the Bible from Clare, opened it, and started skimming. "Here it is. Shall I read, while you hold the seeds up?"

"What about me?" cried Dante.

Lily took one seed and placed it in Dante's hand. The second seed she placed into Clare's cupped hands. "Two seeds," she said. "Two pairs of hands."

She began reading, "God said, 'Let the land produce vegetation: seed-bearing plants and trees on the land that bear fruit with seed in it, according to their various kinds.' And it was so. The land produced vegetation: plants bearing seed according to their kinds and trees bearing fruits with the seed in it according to their kinds. And God saw it was good.

"Amen," finished Lily, doing the sign of the cross for extra emphasis, as she had seen on the Monitor.

"Amen," echoed the other two.

"God bless these and make them grow!" shouted Dante.

"You know we are only planting the one at first," Clare reminded him.

"I know. But someday it will get its time to grow. And in case we forget, it will already be blessed."

"Good plan," Lily said, winking.

Clare handed her seed to Lily. She took the spare blessed seed from Dante, placed it carefully in its tiny envelope, and then back into her shoe. Lily handed back the other seed and began reading the notes aloud as Clare followed instructions.

"Place the seed atop the soil. Gently poke it down

into the soil, no farther than up to your knuckle. Firm the soil with your hand. Water. Put in a warm place. If you can place it *on top of* something warm, this is even better." She stopped reading. The seed had been pushed under the soil and firmed.

"Didn't she say to water it with a spray bottle or something gentle at first?" Clare asked.

Lily scanned her notes. "Yes, or the soil and seed could wash away. It's down here, later on."

Dante was already out the door. He was back in a moment with the water bottle Mama used to spray her frizzy hair.

"Perfect," said Lily.

Next, the children positioned the pot as close to the heater as they could. Then they sat and looked at it for awhile. It's not that they expected anything to happen right away. They simply felt proud of their accomplishment.

Even though there was no miracle yet, they had just planted a seed for the first time in their lives. They, themselves, children only, had dared to grow food. They were continuing a tradition humans had done for millennia. It was an awesome moment, and the silence before them was holy.

14

CHANGE THE FUTURE

When she got home from St. Vincent's, Ana was on edge. She needed to get outside and do something. It was a drag being old and living alone. She didn't dare go on a walk—what if she fell and hurt herself and nobody saw her, or worse yet, nobody cared?

The thought crossed her mind that she should have a large garden to putter around in. That's how her life ought to have been. That's how it was for her mother. She puttered around in her garden up until her dying day. Why had things gotten so out of control?

Ana sometimes wondered what she could have done in her youth that might have saved her from this present world where seed saving was illegal and real food remembered by only a fraction of the population. Could anything her past self have done prevented this present predicament?

It was too taxing to dwell on. The past was over,

after all. But the future stretched out in front of her like a road to the horizon, and she hadn't given up on it yet. Her actions now would count for something. Teaching the children, and passing on the books and seeds, these would change the future. She closed her eyes and imagined her visions from the past as visions of the future.

It can be done," she said out loud. "The time is now."

15

ANA'S CONFESSION

What about the carrots?" Dante asked, breaking the silence.

"I haven't forgotten," Clare said. "But we must wait until no one sees us."

They cleaned up the mess they had made and watched a few Monitor shows. Lily called her mother to let her know she'd be staying at Clare's later than usual.

Just before dark, when shadows outnumbered citizens, the children began ambling around the small yarded complex: Dante, toy trucks tucked under his arms; Clare, carrying the seed envelope in her back pocket; and Lily, clutching her notebook.

While Lily silently reviewed notes, Dante roughed up the ground with his toys, pretending to play. They quickly blessed the seeds, and Clare let Lily do the honor of sowing them. Dante firmed the soil by driving over them repeatedly, but carefully, with his trucks. They decided to let the next rain take care of the watering. It was a thoroughly enjoyable activity. The children reveled in their clandestine act and lingered outside until dark.

And then the hardest part began: the waiting.

On Wednesday, the children decided to walk to class. Last time Ana had told them to wear their backpacks. They were hopeful there would be more books, but at the same time felt guilty that she was giving them her valued treasures.

When they arrived, Ana was there waiting, as always. The old Bible sat atop the table. In Ana's lap lay a large handbag. The children looked around. Where were the books they had expected?

"Hello, children, let's get those math books out," she said rather loudly.

The children glanced at each other, puzzled, but did as they were told.

"Your notebooks?"

The kids got everything out, too stunned at Ana's strange behavior to ask questions.

Ana slid close to Clare and opened the math book, her eyes scanning page thirty-one. "Now then," she said, studying the book and speaking in a low voice. "How did everything go?"

The children sighed in relief.

"Quietly," she warned.

They took turns telling her about planting the

lone tomato seed. She chuckled at the description of the blessing ceremony. "How appropriate," and, "Well done," she interjected at various points. She applauded Dante's ingenuity with his trucks for planting the carrots, and thanked them for being brave farmers in the new frontier.

"But, Ana," Lily finally asked, "why are you being so sneaky today?"

"I saw a GRIM man outside the church," she replied, her smile replaced by worry lines.

"Oh, he was probably waiting for us," said Clare matter-of-factly. "He still watches us. But don't worry. He didn't see us plant the carrots."

The math book fell from Ana's hands and her mouth dropped open. "What? How long has this been going on?"

Clare shrugged. "Ever since I got the first seeds."

"Why didn't you tell me?" She gave no time for a response. "I'm afraid I haven't told you everything." Ana closed her eyes for a moment, gathering her thoughts. When she opened them, she spoke quietly.

"Some years back, GRIM raided my home. They found me illegally growing plants. All of my indoor vegetables were seized and the ones in my yard destroyed. I was fined a lot of money and watched closely for a long time." She looked at Clare.

"Clare, I'm afraid they may have started following you because they saw the two of us together in the park. If they suspect you kids are meeting me here, you could be in jeopardy. That's why I was being cautious today after seeing the man. You never know who might be watching and listening." She shook her head. "Why didn't you tell me they've been following you?" she said again.

"It didn't seem like that big a deal," Clare said.

"Dearhearts, we may not be able to meet here much longer."

Her words hit the children like pellets of cold, hard hail. They had learned so much, and yet there was more to learn. The seeds had not yet sprouted.

"But, Ana," Clare said, "we need you, you ..." She didn't know how to put it into words.

"You can't leave us now," Dante finished.

"I don't intend to. But you do understand it's risky. It must always appear that you are studying schoolwork and I'm just a volunteer. And you must be *very* careful when I give you anything."

"Are there more books?" Dante whispered.

"Yes, dear, I can help you with that," Ana said in her loud voice again, taking hold of Dante's book. She spoke quickly, but quietly. "I never told you this, but I'm a Seed Saver."

The children exchanged knowing glances.

"Over the past thirty-five years I have been growing vegetables and saving the seeds. At times, I've managed to meet other Seed Savers from around the country and trade with them. GRIM didn't find the seeds during the raid or prove my connection as a Seed Saver—although I believe that's what they were after. I want to give you kids my seeds to continue the tradition until a time when it won't have to be done in secret. But you must be extremely careful."

"Seeds?" gasped Lily. "More seeds?" The children looked at each other in disbelief.

"How many are we talking about?" Clare asked.

"A lot."

Ana reached into her bag and began pulling out brown paper packages of various sizes, folded and taped, neat letters printed in black on each one. BASIL, THYME, CARROT, PEPPER, TOMATO, LETTUCE, CHIVES, SPINACH, MELON, CUCUMBER. The list went on.

"These," she said, "are most of them. But I couldn't bring them all. The largest seeds—beans, peas, corn, and the like—were just too much. I'll try to bring them next time."

The children started to admire the packets, but Ana tucked the seeds into their bags quickly, speaking all the while. "You mustn't eat all your Sweeties at once," she said, in case anyone glanced their way. Although longing to touch and read each labeled packet, the children played along, helping hide away their newest treasures.

"Most of these seeds are fresh," Ana said. "I usually plant as much of everything as I can. I eat fresh produce and freeze a little, but my first priority is to save new seeds for the next year.

"Please listen, even though I know you don't understand some of what I'm saying." She picked up a math book and looked at it, as if reading. "You are only beginning, so I don't want you to do everything this year. The seeds will last a year or more and still be fine. I'm giving them to you now because I don't know how many more years I might be around—"

She held up her hand, as the children opened their mouths to protest, "—no," she said, "listen. I am an old woman. I may have another ten years in me, but I may not. It's my duty to the future to pass these seeds on for safe-keeping. It was always my plan to bring you these seeds today. I thought it would help take your minds off waiting for your seeds to sprout.

"But seeing GRIM here, and knowing *they saw me* has made me worry. If they recognize me, if they put together that you kids and I are meeting, we could be in trouble. What I'm trying to say is—we may have less time together than I'd envisioned. But even if we need to adjust, I believe you are ready. You have enough knowledge to carry on."

She looked up from the book. Three pairs of sad eyes looked back at her.

"What, what do you mean?" Dante asked.

"As I said, I had planned to surprise you with the seeds today. We have been having so much fun." She smiled warmly and met each child's eyes. "But perhaps I've been living in a dream, thinking we were safe here. We need to be more cautious. There are things I still need to do. I need to let you know how to contact other Seed Savers. I'd like you to have all my books. I've taught you hardly anything about harvesting and preservation ..." Her voice drifted off, defeated.

"I'm not sure where to go from here, anymore. Now that I know we're being watched."

"But what if you're wrong!" Clare said, almost too loudly. She lowered her voice. "What if GRIM doesn't remember you? What if they're just here waiting for us because they always follow us around? We can keep doing what we've been doing. You can teach us everything. And you're not going to die! You're really healthy. You're healthier than lots of people younger than you, I bet."

"Thank you, dear," Ana answered. "Let's hope I am wrong. But, Clare, think about this: What if I'm not?"

16

🌼

ANA SAYS GOODBYE

t was an emotional session at St. Vincent's. In the end, Ana's reasoning won out. It was decided the children would miss tutoring on their next scheduled day. Ana would come and work with the other kids. They would meet once more after that, and then not return until the tomato plant sprouted. The kids were depressed thinking about it, but Ana had insisted. She believed if GRIM caught her instructing the children in horticulture, all would be lost.

Walking home in the sunshine, Lily, Clare, and Dante felt as if a party they had been looking forward to had been canceled. Although they had been ecstatic about the new seeds, the excitement was dampened by the fact that Ana no longer felt it was safe to meet. Then, too, was the reason behind giving away her precious seeds and books—in preparation for, well, her death.

"Do you really think Ana will die soon?" Dante asked as they trudged home.

"No, Dante, I don't think so," Clare answered.

"She's just being careful," Lily said. "The seeds mean a lot to her. She's spent a lot of years keeping them going. She wants to make sure it hasn't all been in vain."

"What's that mean?" asked Dante.

"It means she doesn't want it all to be a waste."

"Oh."

"No one knows when they'll die," Lily said. "And she is pretty old. She's just being safe, that's all."

"Yeah, I guess so," he said. "I just don't like thinking about it."

The kids swung by Lily's apartment first. "Come on up," Lily said. "No one's home." The girls holed up in Lily's room, while Dante checked out some new games on the Monitor. Finally, Clare and Lily emerged.

"What were you guys doing in there?" Dante asked distractedly.

"Girl stuff," said his sister. "Come on, let's go."

Approaching home, Clare and Dante made sure to stroll by the place where they had planted the carrot seeds. The kids knew it was too soon to expect anything, but they couldn't help themselves. They had to sneak a peek.

It was torture for the children to skip their next

tutoring session, but they kept to the plan. When Mama asked why they weren't going, they told her they didn't have any homework, and besides, the weather was too nice. She raised an eyebrow and made it clear they wouldn't be dropping out.

At last it was time to see Ana again. The kids raced each other the last block to the church, jostling the backpacks they wore in anticipation of whatever Ana might hand off. They sighed in relief as they entered and saw Ana at their regular table. She smiled and waved. They hurried over, flung their packs on the table, and began taking out their books.

"Let me help you," Ana said. As quick as a wink, she eased some fist-sized paper packages into each backpack. She leaned down to her bag and pulled out several thin books. These she placed on the table and later slid into the children's packs.

"Well," she said. "How was your week?"

"Oh, we missed you!" said Dante.

"Yes," chimed the girls.

"And I missed you. But I did make new friends."

Just then a wiry red-haired girl passed by. "Hi, Ana," she called.

"Hello, Rose."

"Don't worry," Ana said to the three anxious faces, "I explained to the children last week that I usually work with you. I told them you were 'my regulars.'"

"Whew!" said Dante.

"I don't expect your seeds are up yet?" Ana asked in a low voice.

The children shook their heads.

"Perhaps in a few days," Ana said.

"I can't wait," said Lily.

"I'm fairly bursting my buttons," added Dante.

The other three laughed at his exuberant language.

Ana taught them how to know when to harvest the tomatoes and carrots. She told them the books she had given them before would help them and to keep them in a safe place. She urged them to read ahead and commit as much as possible to memory.

"The books I slipped in your bags today are not gardening books," she said. "They are cookbooks."

"I've heard of those!" Clare said.

"They're not like the cookbooks you'll find in . Stores these days," Ana explained. "These books will teach you how to prepare vegetables from your garden."

Dante licked his lips.

Before they knew it, it was time to go.

"Remember," Ana said, don't come next class session unless your tomato has sprouted."

They looked at each other nervously.

"What's wrong?"

"It's just that ... Mama didn't like it when we skipped."

"Oh, my. Yes, that is a problem." No one spoke for several moments.

"Perhaps I should stop coming," Ana said.

"But—"

"I'll still come to church on Sunday, and Clare can pass me a message when necessary. The GRIM men aren't around on Sundays."

The children wanted to object, but they knew it was for the best. It was Dante who finally spoke. "But who will teach us?" he asked. "And what will we study?"

Lily rolled her eyes. "I'm sure there is something you can bring. Don't you have to read every night for homework?"

"Not really. I'm only seven."

"Well it will be good for you," she said. "Bring a book!"

17

LILY'S DECLARATION

hen the children reached Clare and Dante's apartment, they rushed to Clare's room and shut the door. They carefully unloaded their backpacks. First they examined the bundles. *Corn*, read one, *different varieties*.

"Can we open it?" begged Dante.

"Not now," said Clare. "It's better to keep it wrapped up."

"*Beans,* read Lily, looking at a second package. "Also, *several varieties enclosed*."

"*Peas*," said Clare. There was a sticky note affixed. "*Plant early spring if you think you can keep it hidden*." She turned to the others, "Do you think this note is for us?"

"I don't know," Lily answered. "She never said anything about it."

"I can ask her on Sunday. We'd better check one of the books later to see what the plant looks like."

"Can we see the cookbooks now?" asked Dante.

They each reached into their bags and pulled out the books. The first book boasted a glossy green cover with photographs of green, red, and orange vegetables.

"Wow, look how pretty the vegetables are!" Clare said.

Another book had a yellow cover featuring an illustration of a fork, spoon, and plate—the plate loaded with plump and colorful produce. The remaining two were even more beautiful: Fruits and vegetables of so many colors! And all of it was real, not just added coloring made in a laboratory somewhere.

Because the covers looked nothing like most adult books, for a second the children thought maybe Ana had given them the wrong books. But then they started reading the titles. *Simply in Season, The Garden-Fresh Vegetable Cookbook, Serving up the Harvest,* and *From Asparagus to Zucchini.* They sat in silence as they turned the pages, gazing at the pictures, ingredients, and instructions on how to cook fresh vegetables.

The books were well-worn and adorned with spills from years gone by.

Lily hugged *Serving up the Harvest* to her chest and sighed deeply. "Lily Gardener," she said, "you will help change the world. You will grow and cook food."

Clare put her thumbed fist forward. The other two latched on.

18

A VISIT FROM ANA

Nearly five weeks had passed. School would soon be out. The children dutifully attended tutoring sessions three days a week, though Ana no longer came. They missed learning gardening, but their grades had gone up, so it wasn't all for nothing. They had also gained new adult friends, and met other children. Still, they missed their elderly mentor. So it was a pleasant surprise to see Ana walk into tutoring twenty minutes after it had started.

Clare was the first to spot her. "Ana!"

"Ana!" yelled Dante. He stopped what he was doing and ran to her.

"Hey, kiddos," she said, smiling.

"You should see the tomato," Dante said, excitedly.

"Shh," Lily cautioned.

Rose was just walking up. "See the what?" she

asked.

"The tornado," Clare said quickly. "We saw this big tornado on the Monitor."

"Tornado?" the red-haired girl repeated. "That's not what it sounded like you said," looking at Dante as she spoke.

Clare and Lily stared hard at Dante.

"Yep," he agreed. "That's what I said."

"Oh," said Ana. "You'll have to tell me about it sometime. I don't watch the Monitor much. But not right now. I'm here to work. Need any help?"

The children ran over to Gene, the volunteer who had been helping them, and explained about Ana. He smiled understandingly and moved on to help elsewhere. Ana joined the children at their table.

"I missed you," she said. "Seeing you at church and not talking like this is just not the same."

The kids agreed. They chatted for awhile about school, the weather, and what the latest Monitor news was. At last they lowered their voices and began sharing about their exploits in the illicit activity of growing food.

"You should see how many leaves the tomato has now!" Dante said.

"It has taken forever," complained Clare. "I still find it hard to believe that some day it will be as big as in the book."

"And you were right about the carrots," Lily said. "They look just like little pieces of grass."

Clare's finger shot to her lips. In a flash, Rose was at their table, pulling up a chair.

"Whatch'all talkin' about?"

"School," all three answered at once.

"School? Huh. It looked like you were real excited."

Ana turned to look Rose full in the face. "Of course they were excited. They are learning new things, and that's always exciting. Isn't it, children?" she said, looking at the others. They smiled and agreed.

"Hmph," said Rose. "My school is boring."

Just then, the adult volunteer who had been helping Rose called to her; Rose skipped away.

"That was a close one," Clare observed.

"She's kind of nosy," said Lily. "I like her okay, but sometimes she's annoying."

Ana chuckled. "Rose is all right, but it's best we keep our secret in a small circle for now."

The children opened their textbooks and pretended to do schoolwork while Ana taught them more about what to expect from various seeds. Later, she gave the girls information about other Seed Savers, instructing them to keep the information secure in two different locations.

When it was at last time to return home, the kids had a hard time letting Ana go.

"It was so nice today, just like old times," Clare said. "Are you sure you can't come again?" She smiled weakly, hoping to change Ana's mind, but knowing there was no chance.

"No, Clare. It's for the best. And school will be out soon, anyway. Tutoring session will end. I'll be at church. Let's slip each other little notes now and then on Sundays."

Ana hugged each child goodbye while Rose looked on enviously.

19

SUMMER BREAK

t was July. School had been out for a month and the children had never experienced a more interesting summer. Gardening presented them with a purpose; something to look forward to every day. The once tiny tomato plant was bigger than they'd imagined possible. What started out as lemon yellow flowers, then small green marbles, were now sizable round fruit. So far, there were six tomatoes, and the plant kept getting bigger, kept making more yellow flowers.

The carrots, as well, had prospered. The children pulled up a few in curious wonder to help "thin" the crop, as they'd read about. Being small, the seedlings were not much to eat, but it was exciting, nonetheless, to consume something they had planted.

The carrots had a strong earthy flavor, with a hint of sweetness. Dante especially liked how the tiny roots crunched. The children wished they could eat the green part, and nibbled at it. However, there wasn't anything in the books about how to eat the tops, so they left them on the grass.

Clare and Ana continued to see each other and pass notes on Sundays. One day, Clare found a map in her prayer book. *Do not use this unless something happens*, the words at the bottom of the page read. *Though I'd love to show you everything, we simply cannot risk it.* Closer study revealed one side to be a street map directing how to get to Ana's house from St. Vincent's, while the second side mapped the interior of her home, revealing hidden places with additional seeds and books. It was tempting to want to hop on the bikes and ride out of town in search of Ana's place. But the kids knew better. GRIM still tailed them occasionally.

As the summer days stretched long as taffy, the children busily studied the books in their care. Lily, the artist of the group, was already making plans for next year.

"Next year," she said, from her place under the maple tree, "we simply *must* plant radishes and lettuce. Everything I've read indicates that these plants are easy to grow. And they were eaten raw in a dish called 'salad.' It sounds very healthy. Kind of like Vitees, only in their natural form."

"And where are you going to plant all this?" asked Clare.

"I think we could do it where the carrots are, or even those dead patches in the lawn. Or else in that empty lot." She pointed to the lot across the alley. "We could plant stuff inside those old tires. Nobody would know the difference. Look." She held out her sketchpad. Lily had drawn a complete plan of her would-be garden. *Peas*, it read. *Beans, squash, potatoes*.

"Wow," said Dante. "I like it."

"You know," said Clare. "Ana told us about this once, remember? She said she used to plant around town after they raided her place that time. That she would sometimes scatter seed as she fed the birds. Especially when the seed was getting old. She said almost always something came up, and hardly ever was anything confiscated by GRIM. Sometimes they don't even recognize vegetable plants out in nature."

Lily nodded. "We'll be ready. We have all year to study and plan. And next year," she patted her sketchpad, "next year, here we come."

20

AN EMPTY SEAT

lare and Dante missed the last Sunday service in July. It was day five of an extreme heat wave and Mama had had enough; she was taking the family to the reservoir for a swim and that was that. They wanted a good spot, so church would be missed. The children didn't think much about it. Church seemed less relevant in summer. If God was found in nature, then being in nature was being close to God.

The reservoir, of course, was crowded. For the briefest moment in between water exploits, Clare's mind flitted to St. Vincent's and Ana. *I bet the church is empty,* she thought. Although she was glad to be in the cool water and open air rather than a dark, stuffy church, she felt a little sad. A splash in the face brought her back to the moment, however, and off she ran chasing Dante.

The following Sunday, Clare and Dante were

bursting with anticipation. Two of the tomatoes were beginning to turn color. Not red, but a lighter green—almost a yellowing—as the green tomatoes began to ripen toward the inevitable, final red. They couldn't wait to tell Ana the news. As they walked to church, they decided they would sit closer to her than usual. No note passing this time; they would tell her face to face, if only in a whisper.

"Remember that first day? The day we blessed and planted the seeds?" Over and over they spoke of the many firsts as they walked.

"Can you wait to eat a tomato?" Dante asked. He laughed right out loud. "It's too bad we can't tell Mama."

"I know," said Clare. "But it's better this way. She would worry if she thought we might get in trouble. And she would wonder where we got the tomato plant. Knowing Mama, she'd squeeze the truth out of us, and that wouldn't be good for Ana."

"Yeah," Dante said, kicking a tin can, "but I bet she'd like it, you know, if it weren't for those other things."

"Yes, she probably would. She was always trying to grow things when we first moved here."

The children arrived at the aging cathedral and walked in quickly. They were surprised they got there before Ana; Clare thought they were running late. They took their seats and waited. Dante turned his head often, looking for Ana. The organ began to

87

play. Clare glanced around. The children exchanged worried looks. Ana's place in the pew remained empty.

Father Williams preached his sermon, but Clare didn't hear it. She mouthed the words of the hymns and prayers, but her thoughts were elsewhere. The entire service passed and Ana never came. For awhile, Clare had willed herself to believe that Ana had arrived late and was sitting somewhere in the back, out of their sight. But when it was time to leave, she had to admit the truth: Ana was nowhere to be found.

Clare and Dante spoke to no one; they hurried out of the church and across the parking lot.

"Clare," Dante finally said. "What do you think happened?"

"I don't know. Ana has never missed a Sunday."

"Maybe she's sick," Dante suggested.

"Yeah, maybe."

They walked in silence the remainder of the way home; each thinking their own thoughts about why Ana had not been in church. The can Dante had been playfully kicking earlier lay flattened on the road.

Later that afternoon, Clare rode her bike to Lily's place. It was in her mind to use the secret map to find Ana's house and make sure everything was all right.

"She's only missed one day," Lily reasoned. "I

don't think that's an emergency."

"I guess you're right. I'm overreacting. But we weren't in church last week—Mama took us to the reservoir. We don't know if it's only been this one Sunday or not." She paused. "Lily, do the GRIM people still watch you?"

"No," Lily said. "They never watch me. You mean you still see them?"

"Yeah, I still see them sometimes. I always check."

"I don't pay that much attention," said Lily. "But I don't think they do."

"Well, be careful, Lily Gardener," Clare said with a sly smile, "the future depends on you."

"Aye-aye, Cap'n," she answered with her own smile and a salute.

After that, the girls rode around town, pointing out places they imagined they'd purloin for next year's crop. Ending at Clare's, they sat on the stoop awhile, talking about future harvests, and quizzing each other on the knowledge gleaned daily from the banned books they dutifully ingested.

Clare sighed heavily. "I really wanted to tell Ana about the tomato."

"Yeah, and the days pass so slowly in summer," Lily said. "Sunday will take forever to roll around."

Mama opened the door behind them. "Are you two moaning about how bored you are again? Clare, I think you've forgotten that I signed you and Dante up for tech camp this week."

"Oh, that's right. Dante and I have day camp all week. Are you going, Lily?"

"Nah," she said, "too expensive."

21

BROKEN ENTRY

Sunday never did roll around. It was Tuesday that forever changed the lives of the children.

As always, Clare and Dante were expected to transport themselves to and from camp. Though tech camp helped pass the time, they both thought gardening camp would have been immensely more interesting.

Arriving home after a day of inventing gadgets from garbage, the first thing Clare noticed was that the front door wasn't locked. Mama shouldn't have been home yet, and she never left the door open. Clare walked slowly into the kitchen.

"Mama," she called, nudging herself in front of her little brother.

No one answered. "Mama?" she called again, louder.

"Mama," Dante cried, running from room to room.

Clare caught him by the shoulder. "She's not here. I think someone else has been here. But I think they're gone now," she whispered.

"Should we call the police?"

"Don't be silly, Dante. We can't call the police." Just then a thought occurred to her and she dashed away. She came back in a few minutes. "It's gone."

"What's gone?"

"The tomato plant."

Dante gasped. "What about—"

"Shh," his sister said, putting her finger to her lips, shaking her head no. She led him out of the apartment and onto the sidewalk.

"The books are all still under your bed," she whispered, a safe distance away.

"And the seeds?"

"The seeds are safe."

Mama didn't come home from work at her usual time. At 7:30 p.m. the phone rang.

"Hello?"

"Clare, it's Mama."

"Mama!"

"Listen, Sweets, I'm at the jail."

Clare gasped.

"Not to worry," Mama said quickly, as if talking faster would make everything better. "There's some confusion. Those GRIM men sent the police to our place to search it, and they claim they found an illegal plant."

Clare tried to speak.

"Honey, don't talk, just listen. Anyway, I don't know what they're talking about—I'm sure it's a mistake. I have to stay the night here, but things will be okay tomorrow. We'll get it all straightened out. Don't worry now, and take care of your brother."

"Okay," Clare said in a small voice.

"That's a good girl. Love you, and love to Dante."

"Love you. Bye, Mama."

The phone clicked at the other end. Clare wasn't sure what to do.

"Breathe," she said aloud to herself. "Be calm; think." She pulled out a chair at the table and sat down.

"Was that Mama?" Dante asked, walking into the kitchen.

"Yes," said Clare.

"Working late again?"

"Dante, I need to think about something. Can you go back and watch the Monitor, please?"

"Okay, okay, sheez," he said as he turned and walked back out.

Clare lay her head across her arms. She was praying and thinking, thinking and praying. What to do? First Ana disappeared, then the tomato plant gone, and now Mama was arrested. This dream of real food, a new tomorrow, was it all going to end like this? She felt as if she couldn't breathe. And then, as quickly as the despair, a voice in her mind answered. *No, it isn't. You were put on this earth for a purpose.* A Bible verse memorized years earlier came flooding back: "I know the plans I have for you. Plans for hope and a future."

I know what I have to do, she thought. Dante and I need to leave. We must find the others out there—the Seed Savers. Mama knows nothing. They won't be able to keep her locked up. But we need to get away.

She pondered for a moment about Lily. Had GRIM searched her house? Lily had said they never followed her. Maybe it would be better not to involve Lily; maybe they weren't really on to her. As much as Clare wanted to contact her friend and find out if anything had happened with her, she resisted the urge. Clare felt there wasn't time—she must get away now.

Part Two
THE GARDEN STATE

22

*

INTO THE NIGHT

"Dante," Clare called urgently. "Come here, now."

When he stood in front of her, she spoke to him saying things like, "Why are your socks on the floor," and, "Help me wash the dishes," all the while motioning him not to speak, but instead to walk out the front door. Once outside, she held his hands and told him what had happened, ending with a hug from Mama. He started to cry, but she urged him to be strong and listen.

"Dante, I think Ana's disappearance may have to do with GRIM. Mama will be okay because she doesn't know anything. I don't think they suspect Lily. But I need to leave."

"What are you talking about?"

"If I stay, if *we* stay, they'll make us confess. They'll take our seeds. Who knows, they will probably take us away from Mama. We need to leave here, tonight, and find the others."

Dante began to cry again, but Clare could tell he understood.

"I'll miss Mama," he whispered.

"Yes," said Clare. "I know. So will I."

Before dark, the children had stuffed their backpacks with Ana's cherished books, extra clothing, and all the food and money they could find. They waited until midnight to slip out of the apartment and onto their bikes. Not trusting the city bus station, they decided to ride to the next town.

Clare remembered which way Mama had driven when they left town to camp or swim. They didn't get out of the city much, but when they did, it was always memorable. She had no idea how long it would take to reach the edge of town, only that it was a long way.

It seemed like forever when they finally hit the place where the lights ended. A two-lane highway stretched ahead of them into the ebony night. They pedaled on. At last Dante's small voice broke the silence.

"Clare? Clare, can we stop? I'm tired."

She kept riding, considering his request, and then eased to a stop.

"I guess we can stop and rest," she said. She shined her small flashlight around. Deep ditches, dry now, with long, bent-over grass lined both sides of the road. "Let's get in the ditch; no one can see us there, and maybe we can sleep."

As they nestled into the trench, Clare and Dante looked up for the first time, stunned at what they saw. They had never witnessed the expanse of the starry night sky quite like this. Away from the city lights and late into the summer night, the constellations lay before them like sand on the seashore. Dante caught his breath and opened his arms in a wide embrace.

"Look, Clare. Look at the stars!"

"I see them," she answered. But she was thinking how she'd never seen them. The immensity of the star-strewn sky on a clear summer's night was overwhelming. It made her wonder about all the other things she'd never seen or experienced. Being enveloped by nature, the trappings of her sheltered and ordered urban life torn away, deepened her resolve to learn about real food: the saving of seeds, the planting, the nurturing, the harvest, the blessings. Though she'd not yet experienced these things, she felt a yearning and a sense of loss.

"Clare?" Dante interrupted her meandering thoughts. "It's so beautiful. I feel so small."

"Think of it as your blanket," she whispered, reaching over to hold his hand. Fingers woven together they drifted off to sleep—the earth their mattress, and the stars of the sky, the squares in their quilt.

🚲   🚲   🚲   🚲

They awoke with the first early light, the clear crisp air invigorating them, and followed the highway until daybreak. Clare thought it better to keep a low profile, so they soon found a side road running parallel to the highway. The houses had crept farther and farther apart, and after a while the children began to see the large agribusiness farms that grew the few major crops used in processed food. Massive buildings were surrounded by miles and miles of an unknown monoculture.

This is what Ana had been teaching them: about how small family farms had lost out to the government-encouraged crops that were the choice ingredients in the food groups of Sweeties, Vitees, Carbos, Proteins, and Snacks.

After several hours, the children entered another city. It wasn't a metropolis, but it did have a bus station. Clare hoped she had enough money.

23

A MAN NAMED GRUFF

"Two tickets to New Jersey."

"New Jersey?" The woman behind the counter scowled at them. "Where's your folks?"

"In New Jersey. We were visiting my cousins."

"City?"

Clare was momentarily flustered. Of course she would need the name of a city. She knew almost nothing about New Jersey. She said the first thing that came into her head: Trenton.

The woman raised her eyebrows. "No station there," she said, "only a drop-off point along the road."

"That's okay," Clare said. "Mama will meet us."

The woman took Clare's money and handed her the tickets, explaining where they needed to get off and change buses. The children stowed their bikes and mounted the bus. As it rolled away, they sat as silent as the closing day. Dante soon fell asleep, but Clare kept a vigilant watch.

At last he awoke. "Clare?"

"Yes?"

"Why are we going to New Jersey? What is New Jersey?"

"It's a state, silly. I read, once, all of the state nicknames and mottos. New Jersey is the *Garden State*. I remember, because it was like Lily's last name. We didn't know what it meant back then, but it stuck in my head. Things must be different in New Jersey. It must have gardens. You know some of those old shows on the Monitor where they have real food, and we used to think it was fake, before we met Ana—what if those places still exist?"

"Wow," said Dante. "Do you think so?"

"I don't know," she said wistfully. "I hope so."

It took the better part of two days, but the children finally made it to New Jersey. Slowly, they stepped down off the bus. Looking around, what they saw were not the gardens of their imaginations. Instead, what they saw, and had been seeing from the bus windows for the past several minutes, were half-burnt buildings and piles of trash. Covered from top to bottom with graffiti, faded and broken brick buildings grimly greeted the children and their fleeting hopes for a new future. Her heart sinking fast, Clare stepped back on the bus.

"This is New Jersey?" She timidly asked the bus driver. "Trenton?"

"Yeah," he answered brusquely. "Trenton, kid, this is it."

She stepped back down onto the street. Their bikes lay on the sidewalk. The door slammed shut behind her. Dante stood next to the bikes, looking smaller than he'd looked to Clare in a long time. She felt like crying, but for Dante's sake toughened up.

"Well," she said to her brother, "we probably just got off at the wrong stop in New Jersey. Every place has bad parts, I suppose."

"I've never seen anything this bad," Dante countered.

"We haven't exactly gotten around."

They decided to head in the direction the bus was going since they hadn't seen anything resembling a garden on their way into town. They mounted their bikes and began riding.

It was depressing. Unlike home, no grass grew around the apartment buildings. There was a small park with worn-down grass and littered with refuse and garbage. Abandoned buildings that years earlier had been factories of a proud and powerful nation. In the distance, smokestacks spewed pollution, evidence that some industry still existed. But nowhere was there a sign of New Jersey, the *Garden State*.

The children stopped to rest after thirty minutes of riding. They ate the food packs they had purchased at the last bus stop. Neither of them spoke.

At last Dante asked, "What are we going to do now?"

"I'm thinking I should ask someone," Clare said.

"Ask what?"

"Ask where the gardens are."

Dante was silent, then looking up asked, "What if there are no gardens?"

The emotions Clare had repressed for days came flooding out. They took the form of anger. "What do you mean *no gardens?*" she yelled. "Why wouldn't there be gardens? Why would New Jersey be called the *Garden State* if there were no gardens! Don't be stupid!" She stood up, towering above her young brother and looked down at him with narrowed eyes and a scowl.

Dante began to sob, gigantic tears running in streams down his smooth face.

"I'm sorry," Clare said, dropping down and hugging him. "I'm sorry, Dante. I'm just stressed because I'm thinking the same thing." Arms around each other, they cried.

"Are you kids okay?" A voice broke into their sorrow. An elderly man, skin dark and wrinkled as a raisin, ambled up to them. A cane as rough as the hand holding it clicked to a stop.

Clare sniffed and dried her face with her arm.

"Yes," she said.

"Don't look like you're okay."

"Well," she said, trying to sum up the man's character, "we were just thinking about our dog that died."

"Uh, huh," said the man, clearly suspicious.

"We're fine, really."

"Okay," he said, moving on.

"Wait," Clare called. "Can I ask you a question?"

"Go on."

"My family just moved here. And before we moved, I did some research ..."

The man waited, gazing at them with intense eyes.

"... was New Jersey ever called the *Garden State*?"

He laughed aloud. But before he laughed, Clare noticed for a fraction of a second a look in his eyes. She wasn't sure what the look was—astonishment, grief, fear? It flashed by quickly.

"Yes," he replied. "*The Garden State*. I certainly haven't heard that in a while." He shook his head. "Not sure why it was ever called that." He surveyed their surroundings. "Sure ain't nothin' resembling a garden here." The spunk left him for just a moment before he recovered. He looked at them hard. "Where you from?"

"It doesn't matter," said Clare.

"Do you even know what a garden is?" he asked, his voice lowering.

She nodded her head yes, as did Dante.

For the first time, the man seemed to notice the bulging backpacks on the ground next to the children. He reached into his pants pocket for a crumpled piece of paper.

"Got a pencil?"

Clare pulled one from her backpack and handed it to him.

"Name's Gruff. Seein's how you and your family," he said *your family* with a strange sort of emphasis, "is new to town, ya might need a friend. Here's my address—if you need anything." He handed the paper and pencil back to Clare and explained how his place wasn't far from where they stood, gesturing down the street and telling them which way to turn.

"*Garden State*," he mumbled as he walked away.

24

ANA'S PAPER

he children watched the old man hobble away, despair settling in like an old cat.

"What are we gonna do now? There aren't any gardens here," Dante said.

"Do you think there are gardens anywhere?" Clare asked. "I've always heard rumors that rich people eat better food than everyone else. After we learned about real food, I thought that's what it must be. But where do they get it? Do they grow it themselves?"

Dante shook his head and shrugged. *How would he know?*

Finally he asked, "What do you think about that guy, Gruff?"

"Strange," Clare answered.

"But sorta nice," Dante said. "He could have asked us a bunch more questions."

Clare agreed. She thought about the fleeting look in his eyes at the word *garden*. She remembered his face when he saw their backpacks and his offer to help; the way he said *your family*.

"Where will we sleep tonight?" Dante asked. Lately all he did was ask hard questions.

Clare's hand was in her pocket. She was fingering a tiny square of folded paper.

"I think it's time we call on Ana," she said.

"What do you mean? We haven't even talked to Mama or Lily yet."

Clare pulled the square from her pocket. "Dante, Ana gave me and Lily some information. One of the things she gave us was a list of Seed Savers. She made us promise to keep two copies in different locations." Clare opened her hand. "Here is my copy."

She unfolded the paper. Tiny hand-printed letters covered the entire page—information for probably a hundred people painstakingly copied on this one sheet. Numbers and words followed each name. She turned it over. Midway down, she saw it—Dante called out "There!" at almost the exact moment her eyes landed on two tiny NJs.

"I don't believe it," she whispered. Next to the second NJ was the name, Gruff McKing.

"He's a Seed Saver?" Dante asked.

"Unbelievable," said Clare. "Thank you, God."

The children scrambled to their feet. From her backpack pocket, Clare retrieved the scrap of paper Gruff had given her. They headed in the direction he'd told them. For the first time in days they felt their burdens lift and a sense of hope flow through them.

Putting together the information on the two papers and remembering his words and gestures, the children eventually located Gruff's building. When they saw a balcony brimming with green potted plants and brilliant purple flowers, they guessed they were in the right place. The children dismounted and walked their bikes into the first floor landing. Peering around, they decided to lug them up the stairs, not trusting the neighborhood. It wasn't easy, but after a struggle, they reached the second floor. Finding what they believed was Gruff's door, they knocked tentatively.

"It's open," the familiar voice called.

Dante looked at Clare. "Should we just walk in?"

"He must be expecting someone else. But we might as well; he's expecting *someone.*"

The children opened the door and pulled their bikes in after them. Across the crowded room sat Gruff, in front of the smallest Monitor they had ever seen. He didn't look up.

"Mr. Gruff," Clare said.

He put up his hand, as if to pause her. The children waited.

Gruff let out a long, low whistle. He turned.

"I'm so glad you came," he said, "I can't believe you're here."

Dante and Clare exchanged puzzled glances.

"Here," he said, pointing to the Monitor. "You've been reported missing."

Their eyes grew large.

"Don't worry," he continued. "Before I checked here, I checked with the Network. Something about your garden question made me wonder. I learned that Clare and Dante James were on the run. Then I checked the Monitor for images. I was just about to go back and look for you. But I see you've either also checked me out, or are very brave, or perhaps are somewhat foolish and desperate children."

The children stood frozen, holding the handlebars of their bicycles, trying to make sense of the old man.

"Well, sit, sit," Gruff commanded. "What's the matter? All is well now. You're safe here. I just hope nobody recognized you and reported you to the authorities." He got up and walked over to Dante, uncurling his fingers from the bike. "You must be Dante."

Dante nodded.

"Sit down, Dante," he said, walking the boy to a couch. The couch was piled high with old newspapers and magazines with barely room to sit.

Clare broke from her trance. She parked her bike near the door and crossed the room to Dante. Shoving the paper pile aside, she squeezed in next to him, arms folded defensively in front of her.

Despite the awkwardness of the situation, her eyes couldn't help drinking in the apartment. Except for the library, she had never seen so many books—none of which were on shelves. They were scattered and piled throughout the room: on chairs, end tables, and the floor. She strained to read the titles.

Between the books were magazines, flipped open to hold the place of half-read articles and essays. In the corner was the table where they'd first seen Gruff —every square inch of it covered, and in the middle, the smallest Monitor they'd ever seen.

Most surprising, were the numerous potted plants dangling from the ceiling: an indoor jungle. Clare had never seen anything like it. Her mouth drifted open as she stared at the apartment brimming with both life and years gone by.

"Children," Gruff said. "Forgive me. I'm guessing you've never been in the home of a packratting old widower before. I know it's a bit much, but, I'm here alone ... Excuse the mess—"

"Oh no," stammered Clare. "It's wonderful. Plants, books—"

"Mama tried to grow a houseplant once," Dante said.

At the mention of Mama, the children felt a pang of homesickness. They blinked back the tears that welled up in their eyes.

"Are you hungry?" Gruff asked, their watery eyes unnerving him.

"Yes," said Dante at the same time Clare said, "Not really, we ate when we got off the bus."

"Well, sounds like at least one of you is." Gruff got up and headed toward an arched doorway. "Kitchen's in here," he called over his shoulder. "Come on!"

The kids followed.

"You're lucky," he said. "So many things in season this time of year."

Clare and Dante exchanged interested glances. Gruff bent down and pulled two large tomatoes out of a bin.

"Are those tomatoes?" Dante cried.

Gruff's eyes twinkled. "They certainly are."

The children thought about their own tomato plant. They remembered the recent afternoon they had come home to the molested apartment; how they discovered their mother had been arrested. Gruff was quiet as he sliced the tomatoes and set them in front of the children.

"Some people like them with salt," he said, pushing a dish with the grainy, white substance toward them. "I like them just like this." He picked up a slice with two fingers, bent his head back, and hanging the red wedge over his mouth, took a big bite, followed by a satisfied smile. The children copied him.

The tomatoes were sweet and juicy. Clare and Dante had never eaten food that was juicy. It was incredible. Over and over they placed the slices in their mouths and bit down—sometimes quickly, squirting juice out at all angles and giggling; other times they bit down slowly, squeezing, crushing, nearly drinking the juice. They tried the tomatoes with salt. Before long, all the slices had disappeared. The empty plate staring up at them, Clare suddenly realized what they'd done. Her face fell.

"Mr. Gruff," she said shamefully. "I'm so sorry. We've eaten up your wonderful tomatoes."

He stood and walked toward the bin. "Oh, that's okay, there's more." A wide grin split his face as he showed the children his bin full of ripe tomatoes. "In fact, that was only one kind. I have several varieties. Here, try these." He scooped up some small yellow pear-shaped fruits and set them in front of the children.

"What are these?" asked Clare in awe.

"Tomatoes. There are many kinds of tomatoes, kids."

Dante popped the entire thing into his mouth.

"Whoa," Gruff said. "You might want to remove the stem first, little fella." He pulled the stem off one and popped it into his own mouth. They ate several of the tiny tomatoes.

"And now," Gruff said, "for dessert." He turned and left the room, a bowl in his hand. The children waited. After a few minutes, they began to worry. They discussed what they should do. Just as Dante stood up to go look for him, Gruff returned. He set the bowl on the table. In the dish were small blue spheres.

"What is this?" Dante asked.

"Clare?" asked Gruff, giving her the same look Ana had when quizzing them on their studies.

She shrugged her shoulders. "I'm guessing it's fruit," she said. "Like what Ana told us about. Like Sweeties. Like peaches."

Gruff smiled. "Indeed. These are berries. Blueberries. They're easier to grow than a lot of fruits because they grow on bushes rather than trees. Try them," he urged, pushing the bowl forward.

Clare hesitated. "I didn't know blueberries really existed," she said. "I've heard of blueberry flavored Sweeties, but I never thought they were really, like, you know, from a plant."

"My sweet girl, don't you know that all food originates from plants and animals."

"Animals??!" the children cried.

"Another story," he said, his hand up. "Forget I said that." He offered them the berries. "Eat."

Dante put a berry in his mouth. He curled his tongue around it, and rolled it around before biting down. It was soft, yet explosive, as the skin broke. The taste was pure and sweet. It wasn't as juicy as the tomato, but the flavor was so like a Sweetie. He laughed.

"Go on," Gruff insisted of Clare. "Here, do it by the handful—straight into your mouth."

Clare did as she was told and dumped a small handful into her mouth. As she savored this new and wonderful food, Clare remembered the night she and Dante had gazed up at the star-strewn sky, the feeling of smallness and emptiness of her life, and she delighted now in this new experience.

"Well?" asked Gruff expectantly.

"They're wonderful—where did you get them?"

Gruff nodded his head toward the archway. "Come with me."

He led them out of the kitchen and back through the main room. He disappeared behind some curtains, to a sliding glass door that opened onto the balcony they'd seen from the street. His sitting room, thick with plants, was nothing compared to this. The balcony exploded in vegetation. Plants were everywhere—on the floor, on benches, on the wide railing. Pots were stacked and tiered. Gruff pointed to some large containers bearing three bushes. Each bush held the little round blueberries; a few of the berries were green. He plucked off a large, dark blue one and popped it into his mouth.

"Blueberry," he said simply.

Clare's mouth dropped open in disbelief. Her eyes darted from the floor to the benches and railing. "You grow these blueberries right here? But—"

Before she could finish, however, she noticed the wall of the apartment building. Trellises of lush, verdant vines bearing large, green tomatoes covered the wall. Her hand flew to her mouth.

"Those are your tomatoes?" Dante asked, having

seen them.

"Sure are."

"But, but how can you have them out here in the open?" Clare asked in astonishment.

Gruff motioned the children to sit on the porcelain stools and wooden boxes. He sighed. "Nobody really cares about New Jersey. Least of all this town, or this part of town. Perhaps you noticed." He waved his hand toward the dilapidated and vacant neighborhood.

"Just to be safe, I pick the tomatoes before they turn red and let them ripen inside. Not that it matters. Not much enforcement goes on around here. For anything. Hmph." He stared straight ahead. "Society has given up on us."

The children listened in quiet disbelief as Gruff told his story. "In the beginning, when the regulations for urban gardening first began, we were careful. But the truth is," he paused, and his eyes grew hard, "by the time seed saving and gardening became illegal, most folk didn't notice *or care*. They had grown used to processed and packaged food. In time, people forgot food came from living things."

He shrugged his shoulders. "Most folk, 'specially city folk, knew nothing about producing their own food. But some of us weren't so easy to get rid of. We went underground, so to speak." The light was coming back to his face. "We networked. We called each other *Seed Savers*."

He smiled. "We're strong in number, even now. Yes, Clare, I used to be careful about where I grew my food. And then one day it dawned on me: Nobody has plant knowledge anymore. People see a bush, a tree, a flower, but they don't know the names. They don't know what's edible and what's not.

"GRIM doesn't drive through this neighborhood. Little by little, I began replacing my ornamentals with edibles. And nobody noticed." He let out a long sigh and stuck out his lower lip.

The children's eyes wandered from the storyteller to the plants, bushes, and even trees, on the balcony. "All of these make food?" Dante asked.

"Nah. Some are just flowers. But they are flowers you can eat," he said, winking.

"What!?"

"Sure," said Gruff. He reached over and picked a bright red flower and handed it to the boy.

"Try this."

Dante held the soft flower in his hand. He giggled and then bit into it. He chewed it up.

"Well?" Clare asked, "How is it?"

"Good," said Dante. "Have one yourself."

"Are the yellow ones okay to eat?" she asked Gruff.

"Certainly. Be my guest."

Lifting it to her nose, Clare first smelled the flower. Then she brought it to her lips and nibbled a tiny piece. It wasn't bad. A little spicy, but not unpleasant. If she had known, she might have described it as a slightly nutty flavor.

25

❦

GARDEN IN THE SKY

"Mr. Gruff," asked Clare, "will you teach us?"

"I'll do what I can. But I think you kids could use a shower and a good night's sleep before we talk more —am I right?"

Clare and Dante looked at each other. Yes, Gruff was right, they could wait.

Gruff left them on the balcony and returned inside to make room for them.

That night the children slept long and deep. Dante dreamt of juicy, red tomatoes and sweet, tangy blueberries, while Clare dreamt of books whose pages opened to green vines that grew on and on like Jack's beanstalk.

Awaking on the now-cleared couch, Clare was shocked that she had slept so late! A slight sound from the floor indicated that Dante, too, had overslept. She gazed at the peaceful face of her young brother and breathed a prayer of thanks that they'd come this far.

A delightful aroma filled the apartment. Following her nose, Clare discovered Gruff in the kitchen, cooking.

"Good morning," he called cheerfully. "How are you this fine summer morning?"

"Good," said Clare, peering at the pan on the stove. "What are you cooking?"

"Eggs."

"Eggs? Like bird eggs?"

He laughed. "Yeah, like that. It's like your Protein meals. Without the processing."

She sat down and was presented with a plate of eggs and Carbo squares smeared with a gooey, golden-brown substance.

"I wish I could give you some actual bread with honey," the old man said. "But this will have to do."

"Should we wake Dante?"

"Let him sleep. We're in no hurry."

"Are you going to eat?" Clare asked, noticing only one place was set.

"I ate hours ago. Go ahead—my pleasure."

Clare cut the egg with her fork. It was so different than the Protein squares she was used to; the texture was soft, almost slimy. But the taste was rich and distinctive. Before she knew it, she'd

120

finished the eggs. Clare looked at the Carbos—she knew the taste from memory, the brittle hardness. After the lusciousness of the egg, she had no desire to eat it.

Gruff saw her hesitation. "Go ahead," he urged. "I know bread would be better, but the honey is fresh. You have to try it. Oh, I almost forgot the fruit." He ducked into the refrigerator and brought out a bowl of brightly-colored cubes. They looked like Sweeties, only three dimensional.

"Melon," he said. "Three kinds."

Just then, Dante stumbled into the kitchen, rubbing the sleep from his eyes.

"Good morning, Sleepyhead," Gruff said. "Melon?"

Dante was catching on fast about the tastiness of real food. His small hand shot to the bowl of fruit. He scooped up a couple of squares with his fingers and was surprised at how wet and sticky they were.

Gruff again invited Clare to try some.

Dante bit into one of the green cubes. It was sweet, juicy, and crunchy all at once. It was a miracle. He wanted to slow down his chewing, but at the same time, he wanted to taste the other colors—one a light orange, the other a deep yellow.

"Mmm," Clare said, tasting a yellow one, "it tastes like Juice, only better somehow, fuller. But it's a new flavor. And it's so cold."

"It's been in the fridge," said Gruff. "I suppose you

don't have a refrigerator."

Clare and Dante shook their heads from side to side.

"Not really," said Clare. "There's one in our apartment, but it doesn't work. We just keep stuff in there. It's not like this one, not cold inside. This food is really good, Mr. Gruff. Thank you so much."

"But you're not finished," he insisted. "There's still the honey—"

"I really have had plenty," said Clare. "We aren't used to eating so much."

Dante nodded affirmatively, rubbing his belly. He'd emptied half the dish of melon squares.

"Mr. Gruff," began Clare.

"It's Gruff, Sweetheart, not Mr. Gruff."

"Gruff," she began again, "when we got here yesterday you said you knew we had run away. How did you know?"

Gruff let out a long sigh.

"It was on the Seed Savers Network that you and your brother had fled after your mother's arrest. Someone named Lily sent the alert."

Clare and Dante looked at each other.

"Lily!? So she must have figured out what happened. But why would she post our pictures?"

"Oh, no, she didn't do that. I looked for pictures of the two of you separately. I figured if you were missing, your photos would be up, and they were. You knocked on my door just as I found last year's school photos of you on the Monitor."

"What about Mama?" Clare asked.

"I knew you would ask, so I looked that up last night. Unfortunately, there is no mention of the arrest in the news, and the Network alert did not elaborate. GRIM likes to keep its business as hush-hush as possible."

"But Lily was able to let the Seed Savers Network know about us?"

"Yes," said Gruff, "and I'm not familiar with anyone by that name. Who is she?"

The kids exchanged hesitant glances. An old wariness had crept up on them.

Gruff read their fear. He spoke quietly. "It's okay. I'm your friend. But if you don't want to talk about things now, I understand. It can wait."

"Come on, Dante, let's get dressed," Clare said. "Thanks again for breakfast," she told Gruff. She set her plate in the sink, mumbling an apology about the untouched Carbos.

Gruff kept busy in the kitchen, giving the children time alone together.

"I wanted more food," complained Dante when they were in the other room.

"But you ate all that fruit! And you said you were full."

"Yeah, but I could smell whatever you had and it smelled good."

"It was good. I'm sorry. I'll make sure you get

some later. It was eggs," she whispered. "Can you believe that?"

"Eggs??" His eyes grew wide. He wondered how long it would take to find and steal so many bird eggs. Their host was certainly unlike anyone they had ever met.

Clare nodded her head. "Gruff has so much real food. I think we can trust him, don't you?" They kept their voices low.

"Yeah," said Dante. "He seems real nice. Even on the street, I sort of liked him," he reminded her. "Clare? What do we do now?"

"I don't know. New Jersey isn't what I'd hoped. But in a way, it's a little like it. I mean, it's not full of gardens like in Ana's books, but Gruff's balcony is sort of a garden. Saving seeds and growing food is still illegal, but it doesn't seem to matter much here."

"Can we stay?" Dante asked.

Tears began to roll down Clare's face.

"I don't know. I was trying to keep everything safe—the seeds, the books, Mama, Lily ... I was trying to find a place where people still have gardens ... maybe this is as good as it gets. I just don't know." She pushed the tears away.

Dante put his arms around his sister. "It's okay. We did the right thing. We'll find a place where regular people still grow food—look how close we are now. I know Mama's okay. I had a dream about her last night. And Lily has already helped us! Everything will be fine."

Clare sniffed and smiled weakly. She heard a noise and looked up. Gruff stood in the doorway.

"And there *are* still places where gardening is legal—many places. Just not in this country. You're actually not far from one of those places. Now," he said, "how would you like to learn about my garden in the sky?"

The children were eager to continue the schooling started with Ana months before. They unpacked the half-filled spiral notebooks, their pencils and colored pencils, and joined Gruff on the deck.

Clare recognized many of the plants. Lettuce and chards spilled from some of the pots. Herbs, such as oregano, thyme, basil, and mint lent their comforting fragrance to the apartment garden, while the blossoms attracted both honeybees and bumblebees. Mingled with the trellised tomatoes were pole beans—clusters of heart-shaped leaves and long, green, worm-like fruits dangling from the vines. These were Dante's favorite; he couldn't help giggling when he saw them. Next to the beans, on smaller vines, hung round balls in shades of green. The children were amazed at how the vine held the weight without breaking. These were the wonderful melons they'd enjoyed for breakfast.

"You hit a good year," Gruff said. "The weather's not always so cooperative. I can't always grow melons." This comment started a conversation on how

125

the timing of warmth and rain in the spring and summer affects the bounty of various fruits and vegetables. At times, the amount of knowledge the children still needed to learn seemed overwhelming. But they enjoyed sketching the plants and taking notes on the names, growing cycles, harvest, and preservation of each fruit or vegetable. Gruff seemed as eager to teach as they were to learn.

As promised, Dante got two eggs for lunch. When questioned, Gruff explained about chickens. He said he had plenty of friends who not only owned illegal seeds, but also illegal animals. Gruff brought out the Carbos and the jar of the dark sticky substance he called honey (which made the children giggle, since their mom had often called them "honey").

"But what exactly is honey?" Clare asked before she would taste it. "Is it from a plant?"

"Sort of," Gruff answered. "Taste it."

Dante tasted it first. "It's like Sweetie in liquid form," he said, "but different than Juice. It's kind of like eating a flower."

Gruff laughed. "Not bad," he said. "What great taste buds for someone raised on the crud called food these days."

Clare bit into her honey-covered Carbo, chewing hesitantly. "It's okay. But I'm not sure I like it."

"Fair enough," said Gruff. "Even with natural food, people don't like everything. Different strokes for different folks."

The children laughed. Gruff had a lot of strange expressions they'd never heard.

As they finished lunch, Gruff stood up. "Okay kids, follow me."

Out the door and up the stairs they trotted. After three floors, they arrived on the top of the building. Strewn before them were bits and pieces of former times: stacks of clay flower pots lay on their sides like fallen trees; a rusty bicycle missing a tire poked out from beneath boxes brimming with old magazines; a car seat placed precariously near one edge of the building.

But it wasn't all so bleak. Some of the tenants had claimed little portions of the roof—a clothesline here, some flowers there. There was no time to stop and gander at any of these things, however. Gruff walked at a forced march. Suddenly, and without warning, he stopped. A few feet away was a stack of square wooden boxes. A humming sound emanated from it, and small dots hovered over and around the crates.

"What is it?" Dante asked.

"Bees."

"Bees?"

"You've heard of bees haven't you?"

"Yeah. Of course."

Silence.

"Um. But why are they here? I thought they liked flowers."

"These are my bees," said Gruff proudly, standing a little taller.

"Your bees?"

"Yep. My bees."

The children stood momentarily tongue-tied, working on the next question.

"I provide the boxes for them to live in, and they help pollinate my plants. They also provide me with honey—which I love, Clare."

"I like honey, too," said Dante.

They sat on some crates, and Gruff explained about bees and honey.

That evening, Clare and Dante had difficulty falling asleep. The day had been so full and rich. They talked into the night about chickens and eggs, bees and honey. They laughed about the round melons with the bright, sweet insides and the squiggly green beans.

"And how much better real gardens, big gardens on the ground, must be," Dante surmised. "Places with fruit trees," he said, thinking of the stories first Ana, and now Gruff, had told them.

"Sometimes it sounds too good to be true," Clare said. "Like heaven versus earth."

"But this actually for sure exists."

"Are you saying you don't believe heaven exists?!"

"No, that's not what I meant. I just mean, heaven's like a whole 'nother place, like the next step

... it's not like somebody could go there and come back to tell us ... it's more like we have an idea of heaven, but maybe it's not quite like our idea ... know what I mean?"

"Yeah, sort of."

"And the thing about a place with trees full of fruit, well, Ana and Gruff have actually seen those places."

Clare nodded her head on her pillow. She closed her eyes. She dreamt of a garden bursting with flowers and trees hanging full of round, colored fruit.

26

CLARE AND DANTE'S DECISION

After lunch on their second full day in the apartment, Gruff asked again about Lily.

"Lily is my best friend," Clare said.

"Do you mean to say that Lily is a child?" Gruff seemed surprised.

"Yes, she's twelve, like me."

"Then," his eyebrows raised up on the outer edges, "how did she get out the news about you? How did you kids get involved in seed saving?"

Clare looked at Dante. He nodded his head up and down. Clare told Gruff about how she had first met Ana in church, their subsequent friendship, and how Ana had taught all three children. She told him about how GRIM had questioned her mother, and how the kids had continued their activities—not really frightened. She explained about Ana's increased concern with GRIM, and about how Ana had disappeared. And finally, choking up, she told him how they'd come home from camp to a pilfered home and the phone call from jail.

"Your mentor's name was Ana?" Gruff asked.

"Yes, do you know her?"

"No," he answered. "No, I don't. But she sounds like a wonderful lady."

Gruff decided the children had relived enough trauma and not to distress them further by asking more questions.

"Whaddayasay I show you around the neighborhood?" he offered. The children jumped at the idea. They missed riding their bikes and were itching to get out of the apartment. But then a dark cloud crossed Gruff's face.

"On the other hand, that might not be the best idea."

"Why not?" asked Dante.

"Your pictures are all over the Monitor."

The children looked at him curiously.

"Look, kids, you didn't say what you were planning to do, only that you didn't want GRIM to catch you. Unless you're ready to return home and face consequences, you shouldn't go showing your faces in public. Although your chances of being turned in here are fairly low or you probably would have been picked up already. Let's stay here and play games, or read, or hang out on the roof, just to be safe."

The children looked doubtfully at his tiny

Monitor, then turned their attention to his bountiful supply of books.

"What kind of gardening books have you got?" asked Clare.

That night, in their places on the couch—they'd devised a way for both of them to fit, heads at each end, feet to feet—they discussed once again the purpose of their journey. It had been to keep Mama safe and to save their dream of learning to garden, Clare said.

"And the seeds," Dante added.

"Well, yes."

"I haven't seen the seeds," he said. "Can we get them out and show Gruff tomorrow?"

"No."

"Why not?"

"Dante—I haven't got the seeds."

The boy gasped. "But you said—"

"I said they were safe."

"Where are they?"

"I gave them to Lily. I figured they were safer with her. I only have a few of the smaller seeds. Remember the day we got them? We stopped at Lily's apartment on the way home, and you watched the Monitor? She and I agreed that day that she would keep them in a safe place."

Dante remembered. "I can't believe you didn't tell me."

"We weren't sure you could keep the secret. Sorry. You've been great."

He brushed off the slight. "So what do we do now? We need to make up our minds. Do we stay in New Jernsy?"

Clare smiled at his mispronunciation.

"What's our plan?"

She was quiet. Dante knew she was thinking.

"Well," she began. "I had thought that maybe there was a place where things were different. A place where people could grow food freely and not be afraid. But I guess I was wrong. Maybe we should go back home. I miss Mama and Lily, and I'm worried about Ana."

"But Clare," Dante exclaimed. "What about the blueberries, and melons, and honey? Gruff grows food without fear."

"Only because this place is so awful the government doesn't care." She felt horrible for saying it, but she knew it was true. Images of the charred buildings and overgrown lots popped into her head. This was no *Garden of Eden*.

"I meant a beautiful place where everyone is free to grow gardens and have their own seeds. A place like in the old books," she said.

"But Gruff said there was still a place like that, remember? He said it wasn't too far away."

She propped herself up to look at her brother. "Are you saying you don't think we should go home?"

He scooted up to face her. "I'm saying that we are Seed Savers. Lily is out there and she has already connected with the Network. We don't know what happened to Ana, but we can't let her down. She trusted us." He stuck out his fist with his thumb up. "We shouldn't give up. We've come this far; I think we should go forward, not back."

"Oh, Dante," she said. "I'm so lucky to have you for a brother." She clasped her hand over his, and they merged into a bear hug. At last they broke apart.

"Now say your prayers," she whispered. "Goodnight."

The next morning, the children awoke early. Gruff was already up.

"Breakfast?" He asked with a secretive smile on his face.

"Of course!" The children had grown to love mealtime more than ever.

"May I help?" Clare offered.

"Yes, ma'am. There are some melons chilling in the bottom of the fridge. You can start slicing them. Dante, you can take this bowl and see if there are any blueberries left."

In a matter of minutes the eggs were frying, and the children were helping with the fruit. Soon it was time to sit down and eat.

Clare sighed deeply.

"This is all so wonderful," she said.

"What's under the towel?" asked Dante. A faded kitchen towel lay over a plate in the middle of the table.

Gruff grinned with eagerness. "Today I have bread."

"I've heard of bread!" Dante said.

"Oh?"

"Yeah, I heard of bread in church."

Gruff ceremoniously removed the cloth. Thick slices of soft, brown bread overwhelmed a small plate.

"Oh," Dante said, crinkle lines playing across his forehead. "It looks different."

"This is *really* how you should eat honey," Gruff said with a wink.

"Gruff," Clare said. "I'd like to pray before we eat."

"Oh, yes, of course."

They folded their hands and bowed their heads.

"Dear God above," began Clare, "we thank you for our new friend, Gruff, who has so kindly taken us in. Bless this food—such wonderful good food, and help us to bring about a change so that all your children might taste and see it is good. And take care of Mama and Lily and Ana. And thank you for such a great brother, Dante. Amen."

"Amen."

"Amen."

After breakfast, everyone did the rounds, checking to

see how each plant was doing: what needed watered, or gathered, or cleared of harmful insects. They visited the bees on the roof and sat and watched the hive for a time. It was just before lunch when Clare finally broached the subject that was on her mind and Dante's.

"Gruff, we've been thinking about what you said yesterday."

He listened quietly.

"We've decided to keep going. We left home looking for a place where we could be free and safe, and plant and save seeds ... Although staying with you has been great—"

"—And we've learned a lot—" Dante added.

"Will you tell us how to get to that place you mentioned—the place with gardens?"

"Of course. I've been waiting for you to decide. You are so young," he said, "but I'm glad you've made that decision. You must go there and learn. There are classes. Someday you'll return and bring change with you. It's not too late."

Gruff reached up to a shelf behind him and pulled out an atlas. He opened it to the page with New Jersey.

"You will need to go north." He drew a line on the map with his finger. "The border is about 400 miles from here." He moved his face close to theirs. "The problem is that your pictures are out there. You've been listed as runaways to the general public, and who knows what else inside of GRIM. It will be better to take days, even weeks, getting there—if you wish to succeed and not be caught. I can't caution you strong enough, kids," he waved a long, thin finger back and forth, "you must not ride the bus again. You must not be seen."

Clare and Dante exchanged anxious looks.

"Don't y'all worry. We'll work it out."

27

PREPARING TO LEAVE

fter three more days with Gruff, the children were ready to continue their adventure. He had gathered supplies for them, including food items, a map, another flashlight, and a few other odds and ends. Since they already carried quite a load, he convinced them to leave two of Ana's books with him. He assured them there were still gardening books in the world, even if they weren't easy to find. Gruff told the children that traveling by bicycle, at night, would be their best chance for escaping to the border. They spent many hours learning how to traverse the land without being seen.

"Move only at night," he said. "Try to find good places to rest during the day. If you must travel in the light, make sure it is in sparsely populated areas. Wear your helmets and keep your heads low."

He taught them how to read the night sky and how to find friends.

"Years ago, when gardeners had to go underground, so to speak, they developed signals still used today. When you looked up at my balcony what was the first thing you noticed?"

"Your purple flowers!" shouted Dante.

"Yes, the pansies. I wish you could have seen the lupines. Lupines were really the chosen flowers for our code, but alas, they finish blooming early in the summer around here. So we keep anything purple alive that we can," he said smiling.

"What's so special about lupines?" Clare asked.

"Well, for one thing, everybody has roses," Gruff said winking. "The story is this: about a hundred years ago, a mountain in Washington state blew its top. Forests were blown away. The land was devastated. It's said that the first plants to emerge from the ash-covered land were wild lupines. They're tenacious—like us. We, the Seed Savers, will come back someday, too."

"Wow," said Dante.

"So, if we see some place with a lot of purple flowers, they might be friends?"

"Right," said Gruff. "But there's more. Obviously if lupines grow wild or if someone likes purple, that wouldn't be enough to go knocking on their door and ask if they were Seed Savers. The next sign is a symbol of a circle within a circle."

"A circle within a circle?"

Gruff grabbed a pen and paper. "Like this," he said,

drawing. He drew a circle as best he could, and then right outside of it a second circle, enclosing the first.

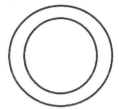

"It's an ancient sacred symbol of mother earth, or earth goddess, and the fertility and fruitfulness she embodies. If you go outside my door and take a good look, you'll find I've painted a small one down near the bottom. Anyway, if you find the purple flowers and the symbol, you can pretty much figure they are Seed Savers. But just to be sure, there is one last test. Knock at the door. If someone opens it, first ask, 'Are you the resident here?' If they say yes, then ask, 'Do you know where Amber Jenson lives?'"

"Who is Amber Jenson?"

"She's not anyone. Well, I'm sure she is someone, but the name is random. Initially the Network wanted to use the name of an early worker in the movement, but it was deemed too dangerous. We've never had a problem so far with these three signs. And GRIM hasn't figured out any of our means of communication. Be very careful with the knowledge."

Gruff made the children sleep during the day and stay up at night. It would be easier, he told them, if they were used to a nocturnal lifestyle before departure.

On their final night with him, they shared one last meal of good food. The children helped gather dinner from the garden balcony: They had a mixed greens salad with fresh herbs; green beans sautéed with garlic and onions; and fresh bread and honey. And Gruff introduced them to something new. It was rich and flavorful, and a bit chewy.

"It's meat. The basis of your protein food. But it's pure. Don't eat too much. Your body's not used to it. And don't ask me any more about it; I don't feel like explaining. I just wanted to have a special send-off meal for you."

"It's very good," Dante said. "I like it."

"Me, too," said Clare. "And it fills me up so easily."

"Good. Because you're likely to get hungry on your journey. Remember, I don't want you going into Stores. Eat your rations sparingly, look for edible plant life, and replenish your supplies when you find friends." His eyes were firm, but kind.

"We'll be careful," Clare promised.

"Yes," said Dante. "We can do it."

Part Three
JOURNEY TO EDEN

28

"THE SUN WILL NOT HARM YOU"

he children departed at dark, setting off in the direction Gruff had told them. He had equipped their bicycles with lights, baskets, and seat saddles.

It was a warm summer night and a slight breeze whispered through the tall grass in the abandoned lots. The sound of tinkling wind chimes melded with the distant rhythmic pounding of a basketball, and the scent of hot tar lingered into the ebony evening. It was a little scary at first, because they weren't in the best of neighborhoods, but no one bothered them, and only one angry dog gave chase for a few blocks.

After about twenty minutes, the buildings looked less forlorn. Clare and Dante stopped under a streetlamp to check their map. She looked around at the street signs. "Left," she said. "This should take us out of the city."

They rode until it felt like their legs would fall off.

"Clare," Dante called. "Let's rest."

"Dante, we have to keep going. We'll stop when there aren't any more big streets and buildings. You can do it."

He kept pedaling.

At last the road began to narrow. The buildings grew shorter. Soon they saw fields. Just as on the bus, Clare wondered what was growing there. It wasn't something she would have wondered before. Before, she had rarely been out of the city. Before, she had not thought of the connection between her food and the land. But everything was different now. In the country, things grew—but what was it and who grew it, and why wasn't she allowed to grow anything? It wasn't fair. Her anger made her pedal harder, faster. In her fury, she forgot about Dante.

"Clare!"

She heard a scream and a crash. Slamming on her brakes, she dropped the bike and peered into the night.

"Dante! Dante, where are you?"

"Here," he moaned through the darkness.

She ran back, her flashlight lit now, scanning the road. There he was, off to the side, his bicycle and his gear scattered in different directions.

"Clare, why did you zoom ahead?" His voice was shaky, and he was rubbing his elbows.

"Are you okay?" she cried, gathering him in her

arms.

"I—I—think so."

"I didn't mean to leave you. I just started thinking of something, and it got me so mad. I was just so mad ... Oh Dante," she sobbed, "I'm sorry."

He hugged her in return, feeling her soft hair. "It's okay," he said. "I'm okay. I understand. I get mad, too."

"Do you?"

"Yes. I get mad when I think of the way it was before and the way it is now. I get mad at all these people who walk around like everything is perfect." He bit his lip and looked away. "Like Proteins, and Carbos, and Sweeties are such wonderful food. I'm mad that they're so stupid and don't know it."

He looked back at Clare, his eyes fierce. He spit the words out. "And mostly I'm mad at the people who let it get this way in the first place."

"Oh, Dante." She hugged him hard. Then she jumped up and began gathering his things.

"Let's get this stuff together."

After a short break, the children decided to continue riding as long as they could. It was cooler at night, so pedaling helped keep them warm. Whenever they stopped to rest, they'd check their maps, the sky, and any road signs they passed. It wasn't easy to see the signs at night, but whenever they saw an intersection or a side road, they used their flashlights to read them. A lot of Seed Savers lived rurally, but there were also many farmers who worked for the government. It was imperative that they not meet the wrong people.

"Clare," Dante asked during one of their rest breaks, "how are we going to see the flowers if we travel only at night?"

There was a moment's silence. Dante waited.

"I'm not sure. I thought about it, too, a couple of hours ago. I didn't want to say anything." More silence. "But it will be okay. This is where we have to trust God." She remembered a Psalm she had memorized a few years earlier in summer Bible school. She began reciting:

"I lift up my eyes to the hills—
Where does my help come from?
My help comes from the Lord,
The maker of heaven and earth.
He will not let your foot slip—
He who watches over you will not slumber;
Indeed, he who watches over Israel
will neither slumber nor sleep.
The Lord watches over you—
The Lord is your shade at your right hand;
The sun will not harm you by day,
nor the moon by night.
The Lord will keep you from all harm—
He will watch over your life;
The Lord will watch over your

coming and going
Both now and forevermore."

"Amen," said Dante.

29

AN ANSWERED PRAYER

 awn approached, warning the children to take cover. Though they didn't feel in danger, they took no chances. They got off the road and headed across a field of what looked like tall grass, riding haphazardly toward a stand of trees. They'd been traveling all night and needed sleep. Although early, the day promised to be a scorcher. The terrain grew rougher and Dante fell. Clare hopped off her bike and helped him up.

"It's best we walk now," she said, pushing her bike along beside her. Dante followed obediently. It was hard work traversing the bumpy ground with their bikes, but it would be worth it for a long rest.

At last they reached the edge of the wooded area. Clare was relieved that it wasn't fenced in. She'd feared that once they reached it, they would find a gate or a fence, or some other obstacle—but it looked okay. However, it wasn't as dense inside as she had thought. But that didn't matter—it was uninhabited and a good distance from the road, and that was the important thing.

"Here we are," she said, sighing loudly.

Dante looked around. "I've always wanted to go camping again. We can pretend we're camping."

"Sure," agreed his sister. "Let's go in more." She raised her chin. "We need to get the bikes in where they can't be seen."

As they walked further in, the trees blocked out the emerging morning light. Clare was thinking how glad she was to be in the woods during the daytime. It was creepy enough now; how much worse at night?

Every downed limb proved difficult to pass over with the bikes. Something moved on the ground, just to her left.

"What was that?" Dante whispered.

"Just a bird or small animal. We're camping, remember?" She smiled, hoping to allay any fears of her brother.

"Can we stop yet?"

Clare looked behind her; she could still see the grassy fields.

"Further in. I don't want to be seen from out there," she said, pointing back toward the clearing. Dante kept moving without complaint.

Finally when she turned, the fields were no longer visible.

"Okay," she told Dante, who was trudging ahead like a robot, the large vacant eyes of someone half-asleep, "we can stop now."

Dramatically, he let the bike fall where it was, and he let himself fall onto a small bush.

Clare laughed.

Dante fake snored loudly.

"Okay, Silly," she said. "Time to camp. Why don't I set up the tent, while you get our food out?"

"Oh sure, we'll have meat and fresh vegetables, followed by blueberries and melon."

"Sounds lovely, my dear," she answered in her best mock British accent.

Clare carefully put the bikes down low. She placed a pack under Dante's head and one under her own. "Goodnight," she said, yawning.

Dante was already asleep.

The children awoke ten hours later, the sun still poking brightly through the tree branches. It was only just late afternoon. They would have to stay hidden for many more hours. It was now Clare realized the importance of the playing cards Gruff had insisted they pack.

In the days before departure, Gruff had shown the children many games that could be played with a simple deck of cards. When she had questioned the wisdom in bringing them, he'd told her she would understand later; just trust him and carry them along.

"After all," he'd said, "they don't take up much space. And they help pass the time." She hadn't realized then just how much time would be spent waiting. They played rummy, and poker, and crazy eights; they took turns playing solitaire. Clare nearly always won, but sometimes she lost on purpose.

When darkness finally approached, the children began walking out of the woods. After they'd crossed through the field and reached the road, it wasn't yet completely dark.

"Helmets," Clare said, fastening hers onto her head. "Keep your head down."

They pedaled down the lonesome highway toward nightfall.

Midway through the night, the children crawled into a large dry ditch to rest their legs and eat. After riding for six hours the night before, their legs were tremendously sore. Both children realized that once their muscles got used to it, they'd feel better, but for now it hurt badly.

"Can I have more food?" Dante asked. They were eating Carbos, Vitees, and Protein. They drank a high energy juice, along with water.

"We need to ration carefully," Clare answered gently. "We don't know when we'll find friends."

"I was wondering," Dante said slowly, "whether we might find real food out here somewhere. Oh yeah, it's hard in the dark," he muttered.

Clare knew he was wondering again about how to see the sign of the flowers in the darkness. Neither of them had thought to ask Gruff. She prayed a silent little prayer. Her prayers these days were like breathing. Short and frequent, almost without thinking, no real beginning or ending.

They ate without speaking.

The children's ability to ride in the dark improved steadily. They used their bike lights when needed, but found that with even the smallest moonlight or hint of dawn they were able to ride with no light at all.

As she pedaled, Clare thought about what Dante had said. Should they be watching the fields for food? Surely the government farms were out here somewhere. The food from the Stores had to start from real food.

Maybe the crops wouldn't be on a main highway. Maybe they would be along the back roads. She knew dawn would be here in another couple of hours; she didn't see how they could possibly find friends. They had passed so few houses, and those barely noticeable, set back from the road and enveloped in darkness.

Clare made up her mind to take the first side road they came to. Surely a little detour would be okay. And if they found a field of food it would be worth it.

"Dante," she said as she pedaled ahead of him, "I

might turn if I see another road. I'll explain later; just follow me."

Clare found the anticipated road twenty minutes later. They turned right. After riding a fair distance, they dismounted and pulled out their flashlights. They beamed the light around, searching the fields.

"Do you see anything?" Dante asked, his stomach growling.

"No," she said, "it just looks like tall grass. Maybe we need to go farther."

They got back on their bikes and pedaled on, shining their lights around as they rode.

"Clare?"

"What?"

"What's that up ahead?"

Just over a small rise in the road, a glow intruded on the darkness. Clare hopped off her bicycle. Dante did the same. They turned off their flashlights and walked cautiously up the road toward the brightness, uncertain of what to expect. As they crested the hill, they saw it—a large farm operation. Several big buildings and a grassy field illuminated by lights on tall poles surrounded a grand home with large beautiful windows. And in front of the windows grew a lovely flower garden: a mass of purple flowers planted in the shape of a double ring.

The children stopped in their tracks, taking it in. Clare caught her breath when she saw the flowers.

"You were right, Clare. You were right," said Dante.

She looked at him, her face a question mark.

"The Lord will watch over us," he whispered.

30

FRIENDS

The children didn't know what to do. It was the middle of the night, but they weren't tired since they were used to sleeping in the daytime. On the other hand, they didn't want to knock on someone's door at that hour. Ultimately, they decided to enter the property and wait in one of the outbuildings until they saw someone stirring.

They were sleepier than they had supposed.

"Hey, wake up, Sweetie."

Clare opened her eyes. It was completely light. A stocky man about thirty years old was watching her. She looked quickly for Dante and her bike. Both were close; Dante still sleeping. The man saw her glance around.

"He's here," he said. "Your stuff's okay. Would you like to come in for breakfast?"

Clare looked again at her sleeping brother.

"Him, too," the man added.

She was coming to her senses now.

"Is this your place?" she asked.

He smiled. "My family lives over there," he said, nodding to another house, just south of the larger home. "The big house belongs to my parents. We farm together."

Clare bit her lip. "Um, can I meet your parents?"

At first the man looked puzzled, but then he nodded. "Sure, I'll see if Mom is around." He turned and walked toward the house.

In his absence, Clare shook Dante awake and explained what had happened. They were a little afraid, but the signs had been clear. However, it felt strange to be out in the light, and a large operation like this had to be government-sanctioned. The purple circles of flowers might just be a sorry coincidence.

It wasn't long before the man came loping back, a middle-aged woman trailing behind.

"Mom," he said, as she caught up, "This young lady insisted on meeting you before accepting my invitation for breakfast."

Clare was standing now. Though embarrassed by the introduction, she plowed ahead. "Hi," she said. She bit her lip. "Can I ask you a question?"

"You just did," said the woman, smiling.

"Um. Well, I was wondering if you know where Amber Jenson lives?"

"Certainly, you must be Clare. And, Dante?" she

said, turning and smiling at the young boy.

"But—if—" Clare faltered.

"If I knew who you were, why didn't I just say so right away? I wasn't one hundred percent sure it was you," she explained, "so it was still important that we follow procedure." She saw the curious look on Clare's face.

"It is out on the Network," she said, "for Seed Savers to be on the lookout for two children traveling alone. Only we didn't think it would be our pleasure to meet you. What are you doing this far off your main route and heading east rather than north?"

Clare, still standing, was speechless.

"Oh, but where are my manners," the woman said. "I believe you were about to accept our offer for breakfast. Enough questions for now. Come! Come!"

Maryanne was a gracious host and fed Dante and Clare a superb breakfast of homegrown food. She explained that although they were prohibited from growing and saving large amounts of plants and seeds, the government allowed them a private garden for their own use. Commercially, they grew a government-approved monoculture genetically engineered to be the most suitable for shipping and processing. GRIM had no idea that while working within the sanctioned perimeters, they also were part of the Seed Savers Network. They had to be very careful.

"Which is why," Maryanne finished, "we can't enjoy your company for very long. GRIM representatives drop in unexpectedly—it's how they keep us in line. I wouldn't want to explain your presence. But," she added, "if they happen to stop in while you are here and see you, we will go with the story that you are relatives visiting from the city—Mary and John—got that?" She looked sternly at the children. They nodded. "But that's not likely to happen," she said with a smile, noting the worried looks of the children. "Jesse, my son, the one who found you, will drive you into town and out the other side when it's dark. It'll cut a lot of hard pedaling off your trip, and get you through the city. You can sleep in a soft bed today, and I'll pack some food for you."

Clare and Dante listened in disbelief. They could hardly believe what was happening.

"You all right?"

"Oh yes," answered Clare. "I'm, I'm just so surprised. We came down this road thinking we might find some food growing, and we found you—the lupines, friends, food, and a ride. We're just ... amazed."

"God provides."

"Yes, ma'am."

31

✳

A CLOSE CALL

verything went as planned. GRIM did not come by. The children seized six more hours of sleep and a tour of the farm. Although the government-sanctioned crop and its harvest seemed efficient, it lacked the beauty of the bootlegged family garden. Here, the children captured a glimpse of the Eden for which they searched. Ten times the size of Gruff's balcony, the garden overflowed with all kinds of vegetables and several varieties of berries; some of which—to the children's delight—were currently ripe.

"Do you have any fruit trees?" Dante asked.

"No, son, I wish we did," Jesse answered. "It's not allowed."

Clare and Dante wished they could stay longer but understood the reasons for leaving. They also felt an urgency to reach the border and find a place with food freedom. Maryanne packed food for them—

mostly the standard processed food, "it does last longer," she had said – but some of the good stuff as well.

"Just make sure no one sees you eating it," she warned.

"Mom," Jesse complained, "they're staying out of sight completely, you don't need to tell them not to be seen eating!"

Around 8:30 p.m. the kids piled into the back of Jesse's truck. It would be a ninety-minute trip and dark by the time they crossed the city. "Try to sleep," he ordered as they climbed in.

The ride was smooth once they hit the main road. The children, however, weren't used to passively riding such long distances. Like their bus ride away from their former lives, this ride felt unending. Despite their doubts about being able to sleep, eventually they nodded off. When they awoke, it was dark and they were stopped. Jesse was gently shaking Clare.

"Clare, wake up. You, too," he nudged Dante. It took a few moments for Clare to realize where she was—a feeling she'd experienced all too often lately.

Jesse lifted Dante up and out of the truck into the infinite darkness. Clare pushed the bikes and their packs close to the tailgate and climbed out. Jesse unloaded their things. He reminded them how to proceed.

"If you ride your bikes the remainder of the way,

it will take three, maybe four nights. It's best to stay away from the larger cities where people might be on the lookout for you. Here's an updated map," he said, handing it to Clare. "It shows how to skirt the urban areas, and the best places to cross the border." Her eyes flicked up at his face. "Sorry," he said, reading her thoughts, "we can't plot the safe places. It's too risky. But you know the signs. You found us." He smiled genuinely at the children.

Clare nodded. She thought about Ana's list, and Gruff. It was enough.

"Well," he said, his hands stuffed in his pockets, "guess it's time to say goodbye."

Dante charged him and hugged him tightly.

Jesse patted his back. "You'll be okay, little guy," he said. "You'll be fine."

Clare thanked Jesse and hugged him. They watched as he climbed into the truck, did a U-turn, and drove back toward the farm that had been a safe harbor. Once again, Clare and Dante felt tiny and alone under the vast night sky.

Wordlessly, the children mounted their bikes and rode into the darkness. They were used to it, now, riding for a couple of hours without stopping or talking.

Around midnight they stopped, traffic all but nonexistent. It was a darker night than usual, with a late summer's cloud cover. They tucked themselves into a dry culvert. Clare took out the lunches

Maryanne had packed: a "sandwich," she had called it, some Carbo Crispies, fresh carrots, and Energy Juice. It was a nice combination of modern food and fresh food.

After thirty minutes they were ready to ride. Dante, who had once readily whined about the grueling schedule, no longer complained; he had resigned himself to the necessity of the task, and had gained the spiritual and physical strength to keep going.

As the children pedaled on, they noticed more and more houses, then sprawling suburbs. Clare, in the lead, showed no signs of changing course.

"Clare," Dante called from behind, "shouldn't we go around?"

"It's faster this way," she said. "It's the middle of the night."

He quietly followed. It wasn't long until other buildings appeared. And with them, large lights.

"Clare?"

"Keep riding," she insisted. It was 2:30 a.m. She had checked her watch and felt secure.

Soon, they were inside city limits. It wasn't a major city, one with roads that stretched forever blending town after town together, but it wasn't a one-stop town either. Traffic lights glowed every couple of blocks, though few cars were out this time of night. The children rode on, looking both ways at intersections, but never stopping and barely slowing.

Movement from behind, flashing lights, shook the children from their trance-like state. A night patrol officer had seen them and was creeping along behind. He rolled his window down and called to them.

"Quick," said Clare, "follow me and don't look back!"

She turned sharply and cut through a parking lot, Dante close behind. They pedaled with all their might. The lights followed. Her eyes searched for any dark place, some place too small for a car to follow. A rundown trailer court to their left caught her eye.

"Over there!" she pointed the way.

They zoomed into the drive and through the court; they took a sharp right onto what had once been a grassy play area but was now overgrown. They kept riding.

A car door slammed behind them but they did not look back. They sped into an open shamble of a carport crammed full of someone's treasure-junk, including half a dozen well-used bicycles. Adding theirs to the collection, they stripped off their saddles, and ducked back out the other side, dropping to the ground. This place was not well-lit, thank God.

They crawled on their bellies to some brambles.

The footsteps of the officer drew nearer.

"Children?"

It hurt, but they inched under the brambles, thorns scratching their heads and pulling at their hair.

He shined his light around the carport.

"Hello? Are you all right?"

He kept talking, as if he knew they could hear him. His voice grew lower, gentle and tender, but they couldn't make out his words. Then, knocking on a door. Suddenly, lights in the trailer flew on. A woman's scornful voice shattered the relative quiet.

"I don't need no cops 'round here!" she said. "Waking us up in the middle of the night. No, I haven't seen no children. And what if I did? Is that what it's got to now—arresting children in the middle of the night?!"

Clare and Dante felt a little sorry for the policeman. Clare worried that their bicycles might be noticed. Finally, the woman stopped yelling, and a door slammed. The police officer flashed his light around a little longer, but then the footsteps grew distant; the car door shut; and the nearly imperceptible sound of an electric car driving away was all they heard.

They stayed flat on their faces under the brambles for what seemed like hours. Eventually, they decided the angry woman must be asleep, and they slipped back to retrieve their bikes.

They were in a bind as to what to do next. The last thing they needed was to be spotted by the cop again, but on the other hand, would daylight in town be much better? Walking their bikes slowly through the dark trailer park, just enough light allowed them to see a burned-out shell of an abandoned mobile home. They went inside and lay their bikes down. Daylight it would be.

Waiting out the remainder of the night wasn't easy. The children weren't at all tired. They really wanted to play cards, but were afraid of attracting attention with their lights. So they lay still in the darkness of the vacant shelter, talking quietly at times, and remaining silent at others.

It was a good time to hatch a plan about how to get out of town.

"I think I can get us back to the main road from here," Clare said. "We didn't really make that many turns."

"Will we go the right direction?"

"I th-think so," answered Clare. She was thinking of how intently they had been riding, with no thought to landmarks to the right or to the left. "Anyway, eventually we'll see some road signs."

"Eventually," Dante murmured.

"It'll be light," Clare said. "I'm sure it won't be that hard to get going in the right direction. And then we'll want to get out of town as quickly as we can. It would help to see a better map."

"What about the map Jesse gave us?"

"Doesn't show a close-up of each city."

"Still," Dante persisted. "Maybe we should look at it now."

"Okay. But we need to keep the light hidden."

The children crawled as far from the windows as possible and covered themselves with the light fabric Maryanne had insisted they bring along in case of a summer rainstorm. Clare unfolded the map and held the light tightly to it.

"I wish we had one of those techno maps," Dante said.

"Or the Mini-Monitors," Clare added. "This is so old-fashioned."

As she gazed down at the map, she saw the road that drifted lazily around the populous area. She needed to figure out how to get to it. Tracing their route with her finger, Clare tried to imagine where they were. She had a pretty good feeling for directions and decided it wouldn't be that hard to get out of town. If only she had an idea of the distance required and how on earth to traverse it in daylight without being seen. She spoke all this aloud to her brother.

"I have an idea," said Dante.

32

DANTE'S IDEA

The children were happy when the morning light flooded in; the dark hours had dragged by like school on a spring day. They retrieved their cards and played a long and gruesome game of rummy. They ate and drank sparingly for breakfast, and reminded themselves to fill up their water bottles at the first opportunity. At last the voices of other children and the whirring of bicycle tires intruded on the day.

"Ready?" Dante asked, fastening his helmet and glancing at Clare, who, like himself, stood next to her bicycle.

"As I'll ever be."

They sneaked out from behind the trailer and began riding their bikes lightheartedly into the lazy summer day. They rode all through the mobile home park, passing, in the opposite direction, the other kids. This went on for several rounds. The other kids ignored them. Clare gave Dante a single nod. The next time they passed, Clare and Dante did a U-turn and came up behind the children—there were three of them.

"Hey," Dante called.

"Hey, yourself," a boy somewhat bigger than Dante answered.

"D'ya ever leave this court?" Dante asked.

"Course."

"Wanna see something really cool?"

An older girl was listening now. She turned as she rode. "Like what?"

"I heard about this place, see," said Dante, "a haunted house."

The two kids who had been listening screeched to a halt.

"Jordy," the girl called to the lone rider ahead. "Get back here."

Dante and Clare had circled around and stopped. The two kids stood facing them as Jordy came back. He was clearly the oldest of the three, maybe Clare's age or a little older.

"Jordy, this kid here says he knows about a haunted house—should we go?"

Jordy was tall and lanky with loose brown curls that dangled effortlessly over his forehead. His brown eyes glistened in the summer sun. A perpetual smile lit his face. He didn't need time to think it over. It didn't matter that he'd never seen Dante before in his life, or that his mother had strictly forbidden him to leave the court.

"Heck, yeah!" he declared. "Lead on, small man."

Dante caught Clare's eye and then pedaled away. Ever so slightly she edged ahead, until it was she who was actually leading. The gang of kids rode on—five altogether now. Clare breathed a sigh of relief. Dante's plan was brilliant. How much less likely were they to be spotted if they were part of a group?

"What's yer name?" Jordy called.

Dante started to answer, but Clare called over him, "Danny. That's Danny and I'm Missy." She looked hard at Dante as she spoke.

"I'm Jordy," the boy responded. "And that's Zach and Jo."

Clare and Dante nodded in greeting.

The children rode on wordlessly, the wind whipping their hair and the sun kissing their faces. Clare slowed and eyed the street signs.

"What's wrong?" asked Jordy.

"Just making sure we're going the right way. Haven't been there in a while."

"Is it far?" asked Jo, who had pulled up.

"No, not too far."

"We got all day, anyway," said Dante. "How about you?"

Jordy's smile widened. "Sure, why not?"

In thirty minutes the children were clearly outside of the city. Clare had caught Dante's eye and nodded.

He smiled proudly. They were safely out of the urban area and headed in the right direction. Now they just had to keep their eyes open for a house that could pass as haunted, or think of some other way to ditch the kids. Dante decided since it had been his idea, it was up to him to complete the plan. He rode hard to get ahead of everyone, then pulled to a stop. The other four children stopped around him.

"What now, chief?" asked Jordy.

"Um," said Dante. "I think we went the wrong way."

"What!?" screamed Jo. "You've got to be kidding. Do you realize that it will be a full hour we've been gone? My mom's gonna kill me."

Jordy grinned apologetically at Clare and Dante. "Don't worry, it won't be that bad. Jo's mom won't even notice she's been gone," he said with a wink.

Clare was sorry they had used someone as nice as Jordy. She was equally sorry that she would never see him again. Her face felt hot, and she hoped she wasn't blushing.

"So, what's the plan?" Jordy asked, looking from Clare to Dante.

"Well, it sounds like you should go back," Dante said. "We should probably head home, too," he added, nodding down the two lane rural road.

"You live out here?"

"Yep, we were in town for supplies," Dante said, patting his pack and pointing to his saddle. For the first time, Jordy noticed the burdens the children carried.

"Oh, no wonder I never saw you around before."

Dante nodded.

"You heard him, Jordy," Jo ordered. "Let's get going."

Jordy smiled at each of them. "Fun adventure, anyway. Maybe next time we'll get there." He hopped on his bike. "See ya around," he called as he rode off.

"See ya," Clare answered weakly. She waved at the backs of the departing children.

33

DERBY LINE

lare and Dante pedaled away without speaking. They were surrounded by fields of a low surface crop, with no place to take cover. It was midday. Clare stopped. Dante pulled up beside her. Crop spiders—small six-rotor helicopters used by farmers to keep track of their crops—buzzed and hovered over the field.

"What are those for?" Dante wondered aloud.

"I don't know. But I don't like the looks of them. If those are cameras then we certainly don't want to show up in the pictures. We need to keep out of their sight and find a place to stay until dark. That was a close call with the policeman back there, and they might be on to us."

"But where?"

"I don't know," she said. "I just don't know."

Having come up with the last plan, Dante felt empowered.

"I think we should ride as fast as we can until there's a smaller side road, and then take that," he said. "We need to find some trees, or brush, or even a crop of taller plants. Like corn, or sorghum." He remembered how impressive the tall plants in Maryanne's private garden had been. He and Clare had run through the rows of corn with childish delight. "And none of those," he added, nodding toward the hovering drones.

Clare was anxious about remaining on the highway but couldn't think of anything better.

"Okay," she said. "Let's try it."

They sped off. It didn't take long before they found a road that intersected. Dante got there first.

"Right or left?"

"Right," Clare directed. "I'd rather not head back to town. And I can see some trees over there," she added, pointing down the narrow lane.

They pedaled down the road until it turned to gravel. Never having experienced a gravel road, the children were shocked at its existence. Unfortunately, they still had not found a suitable place to wait until dark. The trees they had seen earlier surrounded a country home. They rode on. Dante secretly worried about having to ride back on this same rough road. Clare, meanwhile, was concerned about the popping sound of the rocks under her tires.

"You don't think these rocks will hurt the bike tires, do you?"

"Nah," said Dante. "Shouldn't."

They were miserable. At last, Clare jumped off her bike.

"This road seems like it goes forever, but I don't think it's going to take us north. Let's just walk out into the field; it's not that hot today. I bet no one will see us. And those drone thingies have gone away. We need to rest if we're to get back on schedule and ride all night; we already lost time last night."

Dante looked around. A couple of crows flew over an otherwise deserted landscape. Clare was right about the temperature. It was unseasonably cold for late summer, though with global climate change everyone knew "normal" weather patterns could no longer be counted on.

Like a couple of animals, the children nested in the field of grain, covering themselves with the lightweight tarp – thinking perhaps – that like Harry Potter's famed invisibility cloak, it would protect them from harm. As they drifted to sleep, crickets played a naptime symphony.

It was 8:30 p.m. when the children awoke. The scent of dampness on parched land reminded them of their hunger; they shivered with a slight chill and pulled back the tarp. The sky was darker than usual from the cloud cover, and the ground around them was wet. Rain! It hadn't been a downpour, but it was enough to moisten everything that hadn't been covered. They thanked Maryanne for taking care of them so well.

Because the return trip down the bumpy road would be slow and tedious, the children ate just enough to sustain themselves. Their food supply was low. Dante had sampled the grain crop in which they hid, but Clare worried about chemical contamination and discouraged him. She checked the map again before they lost daylight. It would take at least another night after this, and then she thought they would be there: the border.

They would take no unnecessary chances in cities. She had decided Dante's trick of hanging out with the other children had been a good one. It had been easy and was enjoyable, although she hadn't liked what felt like lying. Dante tried to convince her it wasn't really a lie, but she had qualms about it. Still, if they had to, they would use this strategy again.

A tear came to Clare's eye. Thinking about their encounter with the children reminded her of Lily. She missed her friend and wondered what Lily was doing.

The children rode the remainder of the night without incident. The trek on the gravel lane helped them appreciate the quick, smooth ride of a paved road and how much they'd previously taken for granted. Inwardly, they thanked God for the durability of their bicycles which had taken them this far.

The night continued cold and wet, and though uncomfortable, they understood it was to their advantage and were grateful. Jesse had warned that several crops were near harvest, resulting in more farmers and GRIM agents out and about. The cool, wet weather would push back the harvest.

As day broke, Clare and Dante searched for green highway signs that would indicate how many miles were yet to go. There it was:

Derby Line
68 miles

"That's it," Clare whispered to Dante. "Derby Line."

"Is that the place with a library that sat right on the border?"

"Yes, it's still there. But there's definitely no crossing over through the library. Still, if the town is on the border, I'm thinking we might be able to sneak over on our bikes. Or maybe find a house with purple flowers. According to Ana's list, several Seed Savers live there. For now, we need to ride as long as we can before taking a break. Sixty-eight miles will really be pushing it, and I'd much rather try to cross at night."

They looked up and down the highway. It was 5:30 a.m. and hardly any traffic. The children pedaled on.

They kept going until nearly eight o'clock. A grove of oak trees was too good to pass up, especially since they were taking chances being out this time of day. In the shelter of the trees, the children ate all but a small serving of the remaining food and settled in to nap. They hoped the next time they lay down to sleep would be in a bed, and possibly in a place where they were no longer fugitives. It was difficult to fall asleep, even as they knew it was of utmost importance.

"Wake up." Clare was shaking Dante. "Here," she said, shoving the remaining food at him. "We need to get going now. We'll walk across the fields until it's darker. We can't be seen from the road. We need all the time we can get once we are at the border."

What she didn't say to Dante was how unprepared she felt. That she hadn't done her homework on this. That although she had the opportunity to use the Monitor at Gruff's, she hadn't taken advantage of it. That although Jesse and Maryanne had given them useful advice and marked a few "good places to cross," there was so much more she didn't know.

Although she knew in her head what a border was, what exactly did one look like in real life? Was there a line drawn through the city, through the wilderness? Certainly not across water? Were all the trees cut down and grass burned to form a fifteen or twenty foot swath? Did every country have massive fences and walls blocking crossing except at designated checkpoints? Were there guards or dogs or sensors awaiting them? How could she not have asked, she wondered now. Their best hope was to find a friend who could help them. In the meantime, she planned to show a brave front for Dante. She certainly owed it to him. And to Mama.

Leaner and more muscular than when they began their journey, Dante and Clare rode silently through their final night. At the first hint of daybreak, they saw the sign that read *Derby Line, 2 miles*. As they continued on, the landscape changed from fields to an occasional house. Though barely light enough to see, they slowed their progress to peer around for purple flowers. They so wanted help. Dante was praying fervently, but this time it seemed as if they were on their own.

Clare checked the time. They would be able to make it to the city before it came alive, but their cover of darkness would be fleeting. Jesse had guessed that slipping over the border in Derby Line would be fairly easy. "Even in Derby Line things are different," he had said. "People there have gardens right out in the open. The government kind of looks the other way when it comes to Vermont; they don't want any trouble."

"What kind of trouble?" Dante had asked.

Jesse had smiled wryly. "There's always people who think Vermont should secede and join our friendly neighbors to the north. So they get away with stuff. Derby Line is a tiny village at the north end of Derby proper. It's so small I can't imagine that you'd run into trouble. When you get there, look for signs pointing to Canada. Most of the streets that used to cross through are blocked off now, I believe. But I heard it's just with barriers and flower pots—like the dead ends at railway crossings. It shouldn't be a problem on your bikes. Most likely there are cameras, though. In which case, the fact that you are kids on bikes is probably to your advantage. Don't know how well-lit it is at night, but I'd guess pretty lit up."

His words echoed in Clare's head. All the hard riding and days of scant eating led to this moment.

Pedaling forward with the approaching daylight, Clare and Dante glimpsed an ancient church spire rising out of the village. The houses grouped progressively closer together, and ahead of them lay the unmistakable clump of buildings making up Derby Line.

Unlike where they'd come from or what they'd seen in New Jersey, this place was a postcard from the past. It was beautiful. Large shade trees and green grass welcomed the children. As they moved closer, there were old Victorian homes, well cared for and lived in. Clare's heart sped up—a garden full of tomatoes on the vine. Dante saw it, too. For a brief moment she thought they had already crossed over, but then she remembered Jesse's words.

Suddenly Dante stopped his bike and darted behind a hedge, entering a sleepy yard. Panic struck Clare as she followed instinctively.

"What's wrong? What happened?"

"Up ahead," Dante whispered. "I saw him."

"Who? Who did you see?"

"The GRIM man. The one who used to follow us around back home."

"What? Where? Are you sure?" She poked her head around a shrub.

"As we came around the corner, I saw him. He's in his car over there," he said pointing. "But I don't think he spotted us. He was looking down at something."

Clare's eyes followed his gesture. A cold chill ran through her. It was him all right. She'd know his profile anywhere, and he drove the same unmarked GRIM car as he had back home.

Her mind blasted in several directions at once. What now? How did he know to be here? How would they escape? She reached over and grabbed Dante's hand.

"It'll be okay," she said. "Good work spotting him."

34

THE APPLE TREE

lare glanced nervously behind her. Although off the street and out of sight of Mr. GRIM, they were completely inside of someone's front yard. How soon would the occupants awaken and notice two strange children on their lawn? Still, there wasn't a lot they could do. They definitely could not return to the street while the GRIM man was parked ahead.

"Clare, what are we gonna do?"

She shrugged her shoulders.

"This hedge goes all the way around," Dante said. "I'm gonna explore."

"Wait," she said. "What?"

"I'm leaving my bike with you and I'm going to creep around the hedge. See if there's a place to hide or get away."

She thought about this for a moment. "Okay," she said. "Be careful. I'll be here."

Clare peeked carefully through the bushes. She knew the GRIM agent would be there all day. Seeing him here and now like this was so different from the days when she, Lily, and Dante enjoyed taunting him. She wondered how they had ever been so naïve. She wondered what had become of Ana and Lily and her mother. The despair turned to anger and the anger to resolve. *We are so close, now,* she thought. *We must succeed.*

"Hey," Dante said, startling her. "Good luck." He was smiling. "The back yard is terrific; totally unseen from the street. The hedge is awesomely tall and thick."

"And ... ?"

"Well, you can still squeeze through it to a neighbor's yard, and I think from there we could reach another street and get away from GRIM. But maybe it's better if we hide out here until dark. You know, in case he's got the police looking for us, too. Or other guys from GRIM." His big eyes pleaded his case.

"What about the owners of the house?"

"Maybe they're not home."

"Well that's a big maybe," Clare snorted.

"There's an old kids' treehouse-type building. I sneaked up the stairs. I don't think anyone uses it. There's enough room for us and our bikes. If people are home, they won't notice us up there."

She looked at him doubtfully. "Go ahead," she

said, "show me."

They walked their bikes along the inside of the hedge and around the house to the back yard. There, a small garden grew, and a clothesline stood empty. The place had a vacant look—as if the owners were on vacation—but on the other hand, it was still early in the morning. A sleepy gray and white cat sitting on the roof blinked down at them.

"There it is," Dante said, nodding toward the elevated playhouse. Red potted geraniums, desperate for water, hung from the edge. Clare looked at it skeptically. She turned to scan the home. From where she stood, she could see into the living room.

"What makes you think the tree house isn't being used?"

"Well, for one thing, it's full of spider webs. And there's not a bunch of toys in the yard," he added.

Clare considered his plan. Obviously, the best scenario would be if there were lupines, or other purple flowers around—but there weren't. Second best would be if no one were home. But might Dante be right? If the owners no longer had children at home, would they notice her and Dante if they kept out of sight, passing the day in the playhouse?

What were the other choices—to cross to another street and try to get out of town as fast as they could? In the end, it was their bodies that made the decision.

"Please, Clare?" Dante begged. "I'm tired. And hungry. Let's rest here through the day. We can't take any chances. This is a teensy town. If the GRIM guy is here, he's probably watching all of the border streets. We're gonna hafta find another place to cross."

She knew he was right. Up the steps they trudged, carefully pushing and pulling their bikes one at a time. They cleaned the spiders out, and fell asleep with little effort.

The children awoke with the hot sun full upon them. Studying the house and yard for signs of life, they saw nothing. The ground in the garden looked wet, but they supposed an automated system had done the work.

"Look," Dante whispered excitedly. For the first time, they noticed a tree bending low with fruit.

"I think those are apples." Clare said.

"I thought apples were red."

"They can be different colors, I think. And besides, they have some red on them."

Dante's stomach growled. "I'm getting one," he declared.

Clare gripped his arm.

"It's okay. Have you seen anyone except the cat?"

"But it's their backyard, Dant."

"They're not home," he argued. He broke loose and scrambled down the steps. Most of the apples were out of reach, but a few lay on the ground. He picked one up and dusted it off. His experience with real food had been so minimal, he wasn't exactly sure what to do. Would it need sliced, like a melon? His knife was in his pack. It did seem rather hard. He recalled Ana's story about the peach and biting into it. He decided to give it a try. After all, hadn't he heard stories involving apples? Weren't the people in the old fairy tales always getting into trouble biting into apples? He lifted the apple up to his mouth, a hint of fruity fragrance teasing his nostrils. He bit.

Crunch. It was crispy and loud. Juice sprayed at all angles. Sweet, tart, and flavors he couldn't describe, hit him all at once. He chewed the bite and swallowed.

"Wow!" he called out. He voraciously bit again and again. He picked up two more from the ground and jumped to pick another from the tree. Clare watched nervously, urging him back to their hiding spot. At last, loaded with apples, he returned.

"What's the matter with you? What if someone saw you?"

He ignored her, instead pushing the reddest apple into her hand. "Eat this. It's like nothing you've ever tasted."

Her bite sent the sticky spray flying at Dante. He laughed.

"Great, huh? It's worth it, Clare."

Clare knew he meant more than the juicy sweetness of the apple. She knew he meant their association with Ana, their loss of home, the hardship they had endured. She knew as she tasted the forbidden fruit that he meant it would all be worth it if they could bring back real food to the people.

35

SUMMER SUNSHINE

he children devoured apples until their stomachs could hold no more. They found a water spigot and filled their bottles. They reviewed the notes they'd taken and consulted their maps.

"When it is very dark," Clare said, "we'll head out of the village. We'll go cross-country from here on out. No streets. There's a lot of farmland and wooded areas. That way's north," she said pointing. "We'll try to keep situated in the right direction. Eventually we will cross over. They can't possibly be watching everywhere." Although she didn't know if this were true, she knew it was better to convey a strong plan. Her brother nodded in agreement.

Unable to sleep, the children retrieved the well-worn deck of cards and played to pass the time. After that, they napped away a few more hours. When the darkness began to hint its arrival, the children repacked their things, held hands, and prayed together. Clare took out the Bible and selected some favorite passages to read: Psalm 23 and Proverbs 3: 5-6.

" ... and He will make your paths straight," she ended, finishing with a short prayer.

"And bless Mama, and Lily, and Ana," Dante added.

Accomplished now, at seeing in the dark, the children crept down the stairs without their lights. As flexible as mice, they squeezed through the shrubs into a neighbor's yard, and then down an alley. It didn't take long to reach a field of sharp, stubbly straw left from the harvest. They hopped on their bikes and pedaled west.

Once away from the village, they returned to their northern trek. The farmland was a bumpy ride, but they kept going, sometimes jumping off and walking. The houses and barns they passed were relatively quiet, but whenever they saw machines doing night work, they steered clear.

Always they hoped to see signs of friends. And always Clare wondered if they had arrived at the border, and how or if they would know.

Up ahead, a growing darkness loomed in the sometimes moonlit night. A forest stretched from east to west seemingly without beginning or end. The children stopped and stood, staring. They had never seen so many trees.

"The border has to be in there," Clare said. She looked at her brother. "We're going in."

"I'm not afraid," he replied. "Even though I walk through the valley of the shadow of death, I will fear no evil, for thou art with me."

Inside the shadowland of trees, the children flicked on their headlamps. They were walking their bikes now, though the woods were not as thick as they had seemed from the outside. Every twig that snapped under their feet was too loud in the penetrating stillness of the night. Their noisiness in the quiet forest amplified their sense of distress.

They had walked for close to an hour when Clare stopped. "Look," she said. "Do you see it?"

Up ahead stretched a twenty-foot wide strip clear of all trees and brush. "That must be it. The border."

Both children stood and stared, not moving a muscle. They would be out in the open, exposed for anyone who might be watching. All of the movie scenes of booby traps, alarms, and men with guns flooded their minds.

"It's not really that big," Clare said, seeking to give herself and her brother courage.

"It's not lit up," added Dante.

They turned off their headlamps. Dante whispered, "But what if there is something in the ground, like a motion detector or a weight sensor? And how far do we need to get on the other side to

191

escape if we do set something off?"

They stood for awhile, silently pondering these questions, and praying without realizing or giving voice to it.

"Should we take our bikes?" Clare asked. "Or would we be better off on foot?"

"The bikes are faster."

Nodding, Clare took a deep breath and let it out again. They did the sign of the cross, hopped on their bikes, and pedaled for all they were worth. Just at the midpoint of the shorn wilderness, sirens sounded.

"Ride!" shouted Dante, adrenaline coursing through his young body.

The blaring of the alarm became a resounding heartbeat in Clare's head. They kept pedaling, trying to get as far away as possible; imagining the blue flashing lights of the border patrol piercing the darkness around them at any moment.

But the lights never came, and the sirens faded in the distance as the children kept riding. Neither child spoke. Both had turned on their flashlights to light the way in front lest the turf change abruptly, causing them to crash.

The trees grew less tall as they continued on, and a nearly full moon shone down, sometimes obscured by clouds, but other times threatening to expose them. Overly focused on the way in front of them, and panicked, the children had not noticed the gradual change in their surroundings. What had been a forest had melded into more manicured trees. It was only now, as the moon cast its glow and the alarm was faint, that the children's hearts calmed and they noticed how smooth the ground was, how the trees were evenly spaced. They held their lights up and out, less afraid, and curious of their surroundings.

Both children hit the brakes. Straddling their bikes in the moonlight, they slowly panned all the way around with their flashlights. They couldn't believe their eyes. From every tree hung beautiful apples. A few trees of one color and then some of another. Red, yellow, green.

"An apple forest," breathed Dante.

Clare laughed. "I don't think that's what you call it," she said. "But, yeah, when did this happen?"

Dante approached a tree hanging full of crimson-colored fruit. He tugged on an apple, but it held tightly to the branch.

A fluty voice cut through the night. "You need to lift up on it."

Dante pulled back, as if bitten by a snake. Clare turned off her light, and looked toward the voice. A girl not much older than they, stepped out from behind a tree. She wore denim bib-overalls. Her brown hair, knitted in two long braids, danced as she loped toward them. A red baseball cap was pulled snugly over her bangs.

"I'm Firefly," she said. "Welcome to Canada."

"But—how—who are you?" Clare stammered.

"I just told you, I'm Firefly. We've been expecting you." She saw the look of fear Clare and Dante exchanged. "Don't worry, I'm a friend. I know where Amber Jenson lives, if that helps," she said, tossing her head. "Follow me."

The children obeyed. Firefly jumped into a small green vehicle. "Hop in. We can get the bikes later." In a moment, they were speeding through the trees in the darkness, Firefly at the wheel. Their astonishment rendered them silent beyond even a whisper. The vehicle stopped in front of a large, white farmhouse.

"Come on," Firefly called, already striding across a grassy lawn toward the house.

The children followed Firefly inside, a screen door slamming shut behind them.

"Got 'em!" She announced loudly to no one in particular.

A pleasant-looking woman in a night gown appeared. "You found them?" she asked, smiling.

"Wasn't so hard," Firefly said. "But they were pretty quiet and kept their lights down at first."

The children were told to sit and served real food without being asked. They weren't sure what everything was, but they ate it gladly.

It was explained to them that Firefly's family, like many families on the border, were friends of the Seed Savers Movement and had been alerted of two children on the run. When border sensors near their farm tripped, family members had gone out to look for them. It was a familiar drill.

Dante was about to ask more about the sensor when he noticed Firefly lift something from a bowl on the counter. He was sure it wasn't an apple. It was very round. She rubbed the red and yellow ball on her shirt.

She saw him staring. "Helps with the fuzz."

Firefly raised the fruit to her mouth and bit. Bright yellow flesh confirmed that it was not an apple. Juice dribbled down her chin.

"Firefly," her mother chastised, "eat that over the sink."

"Excuse me," Clare finally put into words what they both were thinking, "is that a—a peach?"

"Yeah, good one, too," Firefly said with her mouth full. "Want one?" She set the bowl in front of them.

Gently, Clare and Dante reached out their hands to grasp the tender and fuzzy fruit.

"So soft!" exclaimed Clare.

"You might want to peel it," Firefly's mother said. "Not everyone eats them like Firefly."

"No, it's okay, I'll try it with the skin on. A friend once told me about peaches."

Clare closed her eyes and thought of Ana.

"We made it, Ana," she whispered, taking her first bite of summer sunshine.

END OF BOOK ONE

Don't miss

LILY

SEED SAVERS 2

by S. Smith

After her friends disappear amid mysterious circumstances, thirteen-year-old Lily sets out to discover more about the underground organization with which they were involved.

Her investigation unearths a disturbing secret from her own past, unsettling her world even more. In the meantime, Lily makes a new friend and falls for a mysterious young man even as she remains unsure whom to trust.

As her world crashes down around her, Lily must decide what to do next.

MESSAGE FROM THE AUTHOR

Thank you!

I hope you enjoyed reading *Treasure*. To keep current with new books in the series, sign up for my email newsletter at http://AuthorSSmith.com

CONNECT WITH ME

- Website:
  http://AuthorSSmith.com
- Facebook:
  www.facebook.com/AuthorSSmith
- Twitter:
  www.twitter.com/AuthorSSmith
  and more !

I love hearing from you!

If you enjoyed Treasure, please help other readers find out about it by posting a review. Thanks!

ACKNOWLEDGMENTS

Thank you to

Sally, for her enthusiasm, encouragement, and help in the writing of *Seed Savers*.

My daughter, Ana, for being so excited about *Seed Savers* before a word was written that she was telling others the story.

My son, Forrest, for reading one of the many drafts and telling me it was "good enough" to be published.

My husband, Cy, for putting up with someone with dreams and letting me hog the computer.

All of the family, friends, and kids who read one or more of the many drafts and gave me feedback.

And especially to my sister, Tracy, the best proof-reader in the world!

ABOUT THE AUTHOR

S Smith grew up on a farm with a tremendously large garden. She maintains that if you can't taste the soil on a carrot, it's not fresh enough.

Smith now lives in the city with her husband, children, and cats. She grows a backyard garden every spring and summer.

seedsaversseries.com